LEVON'S RIDE

A VIGILANTE JUSTICE THRILLER BOOK 3

CHUCK DIXON

ROUGH
EDGES
PRESS

**ROUGH
EDGES
PRESS**

Published in the United States by Wolfpack Publishing, Las Vegas

Rough Edges Press
An Imprint of Wolfpack Publishing
5130 S. Fort Apache Rd. 215-380
Las Vegas, NV 89148
roughedgespress.com

Paperback ISBN 978-1-68549-038-6
eBook ISBN 978-1-68549-028-7

LEVON'S RIDE

1

Gunny Leffertz said:
"You need to know as much as you can. The first thing you need to know is that you can't know everything."

Merry enjoyed the movie. Levon enjoyed dinner at Johnny Rockets more. It was all a fine father/daughter night out.

Until they came out of the mall to find the car gone.

The lot was only a quarter full. There was an empty space where they'd left the SUV backed up on a mini-mountain of plowed-up snow.

"All our stuff was in there," Merry said.

"I know," Levon said.

"We'll have to get new stuff." Merry shrugged. She was getting used to bulk shopping for clothes and necessities after a year on the run with her father.

Levon said nothing. The contents of their luggage could be replaced with a trip to Walmart or Target.

He was more concerned with the irreplaceable items squirreled away in the SUV. Over a half-million in cash concealed in pockets he'd made inside the upholstered backs of the front seats. The Keltec shotgun duct-taped under the back seat. The Taurus .38 in the glove compartment. The spare ammo for both of them as well as ammo for the Sig Sauer now resting snug against the small of his back in a pancake holster. And there were the envelopes of uncut diamonds in the lining of Merry's backpack.

"We have to get the car back," he said, taking her by the hand and leading her back toward the mall entrance.

"Why not steal another one?" she said with an airy tone.

"I'm not stealing anyone's car," Levon said.

"You stole this one."

He didn't answer her. He *had stolen* the Mercedes. He took it from a woman he'd left bound and gagged in a Motel 6 back in Waltham. A woman who was going to kill them both for the contents of the flash drive that was now hung about his neck by a cheap silver chain he'd picked up at a kiosk in the mall.

Kiera Blanco-Reeves would be reluctant to report her vehicle stolen. Too many questions about her presence at the scene of a botched robbery and mass murder back up in Maine. Levon was hoping the Mercedes would see them farther south where he would simply roll it onto the woods and let nature claim it. It only got them as far as this mall in Temple Hills, Maryland just shy of the District of Columbia line.

"What do we do now, Daddy?" They were out of the cold and back in the warmth of the mall.

"Are there any other movies you want to see?"

"Oh, yeah!" Merry said and tugged on his hand

back toward the multi-plex.

It was seven-thirty by the time the movie ended. They took seats in a Pan-Asian Buffet with a view of the parking lot. Merry sipped a Thai iced tea. Levon unpacked one of three cheap cell phones he'd picked up at a Tracfone kiosk. He entered the calling card PIN when the phone came to life and tabbed 411 for the taxi company serving this area.

Twenty minutes later a Rainbow Cab came for them and took them to a Days Inn in Camp Hill. It shared a parking lot with a Chili's. They had a leisurely dinner there and stayed until close to ten o'clock. The bar was crowded with customers loudly watching a college basketball game on the big screens atop the bar. Levon and Merry were mostly ignored by the wait staff who were equally absorbed in the game.

When they arrived at the Days Inn lobby the registration desk was manned by a twenty-something man with a wrinkled tie and bad complexion who was engrossed with something on his computer screen. Levon shooed Merry out of sight toward the bank of elevators.

"Good evening and welcome to Days Inn," the guy behind the counter said without looking away from the screen. His name tag read: You're being helped by Dale.

"I need a room for three nights," Levon said.

"I'll need a credit card and photo ID," Dale said, tearing his eyes from Facebook to feign a smile in Levon's direction.

"See, that's my problem. I just got in at BWI and some son of a bitch stole my wallet. I'm in DC for a contract job with the FAA. On top of wiring a new system for tower three I have to spend time canceling my cards and getting replacement identification so I can fly back to Memphis on Friday."

"We can't just give you a room. It's policy." Dale blinked at him.

"Aw hell, I'm not looking for a handout. All I need is a little understanding." Levon pulled a wad of folded bills from his jeans pocket.

"Okay?" Dale eyed the cash.

"So, what's the damage for three nights?"

"Look, I really can't. Y'know, policy," Dale began.

"Six hundred? Is six hundred enough?" Levon counted out twelve fifties atop the faux marble countertop. A wide cloth banner slung above the registration desk read $89 A Night For Singles Every Night.

"Um, with tax that's about right," Dale said, scooping the bills out of sight behind the counter ledge then poising his fingers over the keyboard.

"Thanks, buddy," Levon said.

Within sixty seconds Arthur Hutchison of Memphis, Tennessee was registered for three nights.

Keycard in hand, Levon walked to the bank of elevators where Merry held a door open for him.

2

Gunny Leffertz said:
*"If the rules are stacked against you, change the
rules."*

The following morning, Merry found cartoons on
TV. She kept the volume low and munched room
service breakfast while her father made calls on one
of the new cell phones.

"You have called the Temple Hills Police Depart-
ment's non-emergency line. Our lines are currently
busy with other callers. Please hold for the next
available operator," the mechanically polite voice
said on the other end.

Levon waited, listening for the next ten minutes
to a Mozart piano piece interrupted by recorded
affirmations of how important his call was.

A bored female interrupted Mozart. "Temple
Hills. How may I direct your call?"

"I'm not sure. My car was stolen last night at the
mall and..." Levon began.

The line buzzed then clicked then rang three

times before a new voice came on. A reedy male voice this time.

"May I help you?"

"My car was stolen last night at the mall."

"Did you report it last night?"

"Well, no. I didn't get back there until this morning. My girlfriend and I had a fight and—"

"Make and model," the man cut him off.

"A Mercedes G-Class. This year's model."

"What color?" the man said after a flurry of keyboard taps.

"What color? How many G-classes do you have there?"

"Three recovered last night. One early this morning."

Four cars worth in excess of one hundred thousand stolen within this police jurisdiction within a twenty-four hour period.

"Red. Like a cranberry color," Levon lied. His Merc was silver. The keyboard clattered in his ear a few seconds more.

"Nothing like that. We have two black ones with Virginia plates. A forest green with DC plates and a silver pewter with Massachusetts plates."

"Damn. Maybe my wife came and got it," Levon said.

"Let me have your name and number and we can—"

Levon broke the connection.

"Find our car?" Merry said, busily making a sandwich of eggs and sausage between two slices of wheat toast.

"Yep. But it's going to take some work to get it back," Levon said.

"They have a pool here," she said through a cheek full of sandwich.

"You need to stay in the room until I get back, honey. Can you do that?"

"Easy peasy. Free Wi-Fi," she said nodding at the Kindle Fire on the table by her.

"I'm leaving you a phone. Just hit send to reach me," he said, taking the other half of her greasy sandwich in his hand.

"What if I get hungry before you get back?"

"You know how room service works, right?"

"I have the shower running when the guy comes to the door. I tell him Mommy's in the bathroom and pay him in cash. And get change. There's no tipping 'cause that's already added to the bill."

"Good girl," Levon said and left a stack of twenties by the take-out tray before leaving.

3

He walked to the Chili's and called for a taxi. It arrived within ten minutes. He gave the driver, a Somalian, the name of the Vista Grande Residence, a five-star hotel four miles from the Days Inn and nearer the DC beltway.

The taxi left him off in front of the hotel under a canopy covering an approach that was six lanes wide to accommodate airport shuttles, cabs, buses and cars waiting for valet parking. Levon walked between hurrying valets and porters to a Lexus running with keys in the ignition. He opened the driver's side door just as a bellman was lifting a wardrobe bag from the trunk.

"Not using the valet service, sir?"

"No, my meeting's been moved up," Levon said. He reached out the window with a twenty in his hand. The bellman snatched it away with no time for a thank you as Levon gunned the Lexus off the hotel driveway and down onto the street.

***

"Guess what I'm having for lunch," Levon said after listening to Merry read off the room service menu.

"Are you on a speaker?" she said from the speakers on the Lexus's dash.

"The phone's built into car."

"What car?"

"The car I'm borrowing, honey."

"You said you wouldn't steal a car, Daddy."

"I meant that. I'll return it when I'm done. Now guess what I'm having," he said.

"No!" she shouted from the speakers.

"You guessed."

"Wendy's!" Merry's favorite.

"Bingo."

"Can you bring some back for dinner?" she pleaded.

"Only if you go easy on lunch. I can't have you getting sick on me. Promise?"

"Promise. I'll have the salad."

"Good girl. I'll call back when I'm at Wendy's. Love you, honey."

"Love you back." The call ended.

***

Levon finished the chicken ranch club and sipped coffee as he sat in the front seat of the Lexus watching the same mall lot the Mercedes disappeared from the night before. He was parked on the back lot of a Giant market that gave him a clear view of the mall lot through a cyclone fence. The Giant lot was closest to the mall exit closest to the movie theater.

As he watched, cars pulled up and found spaces. SUVs and mini-vans. Moms with kids mostly. Some senior citizen couples. They unloaded, all bundled in winter clothes. Moms chasing after eager kids.

Cars sounding muted honks as they were locked via remotes. The lot filled to half capacity as the matinee movie times approached. This was the approximate time he and Merry had arrived here the day before. Dozens of cars that would be here unattended for the next two hours or more.

He finished his large fries and watched the lot. Every twenty minutes or so a smart car marked SECURITY in block letters tooled around the lot, a flashing red light atop the roof. A heavy-set woman in a dark blue parka was at the wheel. The second time around for the kiddie car, Levon noticed a bronze Escalade with spinner wheels and dark tinted windows pull around the corner of the mall and begin drifting up and down the aisles of the lot.

It moved slow. Too slow for someone looking for a parking space. It described a leisurely S around where the cars were most densely collected. It looked like a wolf circling a flock, looking for the frailest sheep. It came to a stop in an aisle and three doors opened to allow six passengers to exit. The Escalade sped away and the passengers spread out in pairs among the parked cars.

Black kids in hoodies and Gore-Tex parkas. Sneakers flashing white as they ran to their chosen prey. Like a NASCAR pit crew they moved to their assigned tasks. One to each front window with slim jims working between window and door. The cars were open in seconds. Alarms bleated and honked and trilled.

The driver-side thief moved behind the wheel with a slap hammer to remove ignitions. The second thief lay on the floor to pull the wires that fed juice to the alarms. The car alarms went silent as their engines roared to life in near-simultaneous time. Brake lights flashed and the three cars, all high-end sport utilities, zoomed away from their spots in three different directions.

Levon picked a Range Rover from the pack to follow. It was making a right, south onto Branch Avenue. Levon pulled around the Giant, across the lot and made a left onto Iverson, bringing him to the light while the Range Rover crossed the intersection before him. There was a line of three cars in the right turn lane. Levon crossed lanes behind them onto the lot of a Wawa, allowing him to cross that lot and exit onto Branch Avenue ten car lengths behind the Rover.

He settled into a lane and kept a few cars between him and his target. The Rover sat up high and was easy to keep track of. They were both rolling well within the speed limit. No need to call any more attention to themselves than two black kids in an expensive import might already draw from local cops.

Five minutes along, the Rover left Branch for a street that coursed through a residential area of two-bedroom ranchers built decades before. Cyclone fenced yards. Cars parked on either curb. Some up on blocks. After a couple of miles the street ended at a T intersection. They made a left. Levon hung well back. Not much traffic here. No camouflage.

It was a service road with empty businesses along one side. Shuttered garages and plants. Boarded up strip malls and large empty lots on the other side. The lots all covered in a foot of dirty snow. No plows came this way.

They passed under twin overpasses of 295 and hooked right into a driveway that led into an apartment complex of eight-story blocks surrounded by bare trees. Levon maintained his speed and drove by the entrance of the complex, noting as he passed the No Outlet sign posted in front of the turn in.

He made a U-turn at the next light and pulled into the lot of a Shell station. He parked with a view of the apartment complex exit. Levon sipped the dregs of his coffee, cold now, and watched the opening of the apartment complex for traffic. Two kids in hoodies and parkas ran off the property. One held a hand to his ear, mouth moving. Talking into a cell phone. The pair stood on the sidewalk, stamping their sneakers in the cold and looking north along the service road. A bronze Escalade pulled from under the shadows of the 295 overpass and up to the curb. The same one that had dropped them off back at the mall lot. The two thieves who took the Range Rover got in the back seat and the big SUV took off, spinners throwing off sputters of diamond flashes in the late afternoon light. It gunned to sixty and crossed the intersection ahead through a yellow light.

The flock fleeced, the predators headed back to their lair.

Levon gave them a beat or two before he pulled from the Shell station in a looping left to follow.

4

The Escalade ended its journey in the driveway of a split level on a street lined either side with bare trees and a berm of filthy snow the plows left behind.

6292 West McDougal Street.

It was still light out with plenty of kids riding bikes and playing in the street and on the front lawns. They all stopped to eye the white man in the Lexus cruising past. Levon noted the address and drove on.

He stopped at a 7-Eleven lot to throw his coffee container and Wendy's trash into a bin by the pumps. He then drove the Lexus back to the Vista Grande Residence and pulled up at the rear of a row of cars waiting for valet service, their owners inside taking advantage of express check-in. It was full dark out now. The lights in the ceiling of the canopy covering the entrance drive reflected off the high polish of a dozen high-end cars.

Levon left the door open and motor running and stepped to the open door of the night-blue Ford Fusion parked one lane over. He shut the door, put it in gear and pulled from the queue and off the lot.

The rental agreement was still lying on the dash. He wouldn't need to bring this one back.

Drive-through at a Wendy's and back to the Days Inn for dinner with Merry.

"Did you find the Mercedes?" she asked as she cut her double with cheese in two using a butter knife she'd held back when she put the room service tray in the hall.

"Working on it." Levon spooned at a Frosty and eyed the mute TV. A guy with a receding hairline appeared to be arguing with two other people simultaneously on a split screen. The subject was gender reassignment. Levon tabbed the remote over to a channel showing two guys rebuilding a '76 Impala. He left it there.

"How are you getting around?"

"I have a rental. Have you done any of your schoolwork?"

"We left all the home school stuff back in Maine." She smiled, showing ketchupy teeth.

"No excuse. If you're not provised you improvise," Levon said, digging for the last of the Frosty at the bottom of the cup.

"That sounds like Gunny."

"It's one of his."

"With a lot of f-bombs mixed in, right?"

"You're changing the subject." Levon nodded and set the empty cup aside.

"I was doing a section in US history on Jefferson and Hamilton. I could download some books free on my Kindle," she ended with a sigh.

"Do that and tell me what you read when I get back." He rose from the edge of his bed and plucked his coat from the back of a chair.

**

On the way back to MacDougal Street, Levon stopped at a CVS. He picked up a box of latex gloves, a box of surgical masks, two rolls of duct tape, a bottle of Romilar AC, and a sack of bite-sized Paydays. The last stop was another 7-Eleven where he topped off the Fusion. At the pump he filled the gas can.

The temperature was dropping and a wind stirred the tops of the ridges of plowed snow on either curb along MacDougal. The snowmelt turned into a slick of ice on the asphalt. The streets were clear. The houses were dark but for the pulsing blue illumination of TVs from inside.

Levon navigated the Fusion down the narrow lane left by cars parked along one curb and the berm of snow on the other.

6292 had guests. The house was dark but it was clear it was occupied. There was a Toyota 4Runner pulled in behind the Escalade in the driveway. On the street was another Escalade in black, a bright yellow H3, an Audi Q5 in seafoam green, a lifted Cherokee in metallic blue, and an Explorer with fat tires. All shiny and pimped out with all the candy: spoilers, spinners, sunroofs, bully bars and custom pinstriping. They gleamed with finishes polished to mirror sheens under the brittle light of the street lamps.

Levon eyed the house, looking for movement as he pulled past. All these rides would not be left outside in this neighborhood without someone watching them. A blue haze drifted from the shadows of the recessed front doorway. Someone was standing in the dark, smoking.

He drove to the end of the block and nosed the Fusion to the curb. He popped the trunk and lifted out the canvas carry loaded with his recent purchases. He walked back toward 6292 MacDougal.

5

Gunny Leffertz said:
*"If you don't know shit then find somebody
who does and scare that shit out of him."*

Mo Dat was a soldier earning his creds, coming up
in the crew.

Running errands, waxing cars, getting take-out
and shit like that. His tag came from Tolly always
telling him, "Get me mo' a dis and mo' a dat." It was
a name he could live up to, make bigger. He'd be Mo
of *all Dat* before he was through.

Tonight it was his job to watch the rides while the
crew played the new *Titanfall on Tolly's* big screen.
Through the front door he could hear the shouts of
the players and the boom and whoosh from the big-
ass subwoofer hooked up to Tolly's killer system set
up down in the sunken living room. Mo Dat longed
to be inside with the players, fighting big-ass robots
from inside his own big-ass robot. Another night for
that, after he'd proven himself. After he'd risen up the
ranks and some other new-ass nigga was standing on

the porch freezing his dick off watching the whips.

And Mo Dat *was freezing* his dick off or damned near close to it. Ravens knit cap pulled low over his ears and the lobes were still numb. Two pairs of socks under his knock-off Adidas and he was still having to stamp his feet on the concrete to keep the blood flowing. His hands were paining him, too, and he stuck them through the slit pockets in his North Face to hold them against his stomach, the only warm place on his body. Frigid vapor mixed with smoke from the sherm clamped between his lips.

As he stood and stamped and smoked, Mo Dat wondered, not for the first time, who the hell would dare to touch any of the rides parked in the drive and along the curb. Everyone on the block knew Tolly. Knew who he was. Knew he was nobody to fuck with. Still there were dumb kids. Always dumb kids who didn't know shit and would think it was fun snaking themselves a fine ride of their own. Or tagging one of the cars or just fucking with one like kids will do.

But sure as shit no kid, no matter how dumb, was going to be out on a night like this. It was cold. C-O-L-D. Cold enough to freeze the black off a nigga. Cold enough to freeze the nuts off a snowman. Cold enough—

A shadow crossed a bar of light on the sidewalk between the houses three doors down. Mo Dat stopped his stamping.

Damned if someone wasn't coming down the street on this cold ass night. All hunched over. Hood up and face down. Crunching salt under the soles of a pair of yellow work boots. Some dude out walking his dog only he forgot the dog. Mo Dat withdrew further into the shadows of the doorway to watch.

The dude walked to the front of Tolly's place and slowed up his roll. He moved closer to the hummock of plowed snow at the curb. He was bent over, hands in pockets, looking at the rides. Mo Dat touched a gloved hand to the nub of the aluminum ball bat leaning against the stucco by the door. The dude walked from car to car eyeballing them good. When he came to the driveway he stopped and placed hands on the windows of Young-El's 4Runner and brought his face close to peer inside.

Mo Dat was down to the sidewalk in four long strides, the ball bat held in his fists. He spat the sherm from his mouth as he charged closer.

"Can I help you, motherfucker?" he said as he neared the peeping dude.

He stopped, bat raised. The dude turned to him. A white dude. Half a head taller than Mo Dat. The lower part of the white dude's face was covered by some kind of blue cloth mask.

Mo Dat recovered from his surprise and swung the bat hard. It was yanked from his grip and went flying into the street. The white man's hands were on him. His wrist. His arm. Pulling him close. Without knowing how he got there, the white man was behind him with an arm around Mo Dat's throat. He tried to pull the man's arm away except his gloved hands kept slipping off the man's sleeve. He was having trouble making his fingers obey his commands. His hands felt like balloons and his arms like lead.

Tighter. Tighter. And then Mo Dat surrendered to the pull of his mind's own gravity.

6

Gunny Leffertz said:
"But don't forget that some shit is bullshit.
Learn to smell the difference."

"What's your name?"

Mo Dat shook his head, making white sparks dance in his field of vision.

"What's your name?" That voice again. A white voice. Worse a *redneck white* voice.

Mo Dat blinked hard and squinted, trying to make sense of where he was. He was lying on his side someplace dark. He tried to move and couldn't. His hands were taped together in front of him. He kicked his feet. They struck a carpeted surface before he could fully straighten them. He pushed off with his feet, bringing the top of his head against another carpeted surface. His ankles were taped together, too. He craned his neck toward the ceiling close above him.

He was in the cargo area of a car, an SUV. It was the Explorer parked on the curb. Belonged to one of

LEVON'S RIDE | 21

the crew named Nacho.

"Are you going to tell me your name?"

Mo Dat rolled back on a shoulder and twisted his face off the floor.

The white dude in the surgical mask was watching him from over the seatback of the back seat.

"Fuck you."

Held in the white guy's fist, the single black eye of a handgun appeared over the back of the seat. The white guy wore blue surgical gloves.

"What's your name?"

"Mo Dat," Mo Dat said after a hard swallow.

"Not that gangsta shit. Your name. The one your mama gave you."

"Kevin," Kevin said, surprising himself with the ready answer.

"Who's inside the house, Kevin?"

"Tolly. James Tolliver. It's his house. Bought it for his moms but she died a year back."

"Who else?"

"The crew. I don't know their real names."

"How many?"

"Um… um… nine. I think," Kevin said after completing the mental roll call.

"How long you think they'll be in there?"

"They'll go all night, I guess. Got a new game. Playin'. Smokin'."

"Anyone in the crew steal a Mercedes G-Class yesterday?"

"What color?"

"Silver. Massachusetts plate."

"Oh yeah. That one. Yeah. R.J. and Took snaked that one."

"You remember that one, huh?"

"Shit, yeah. Had this gun in the back. Badass motherfucker looked like Darth Vader and shit."

"Is it inside?"

"Tolly kept it. Yeah."

"One more question for you, Kevin."

Kevin did *not like* the sound of that.

"Did they find anything else?"

"Luggage and shit. A kid's backpack with cartoons on it. They left it in the ride."

"Nothing else?"

"I was there when they come back. Just that weird-ass shotgun."

The white man turned away, withdrawing the handgun.

Kevin dropped his head to the floor mat, sweat popping out on his face and neck in spite of the temperature. He raised his head again at a sound from behind the seatback. The crinkle of cellophane. A plastic crackling sound. The white guy turned back to him, reaching an arm over with a bottle in his gloved hand.

"I need you to be quiet for a while. There's two ways I can do that. You understand?"

Kevin nodded. The hand drew closer and pressed the plastic rim of an open bottle to his lips. He took a sip. Cough medicine. He sputtered, spraying cherry-flavored goop from his nose and mouth. The hand tipped the bottle back.

"Do I need to go the other way, Kevin?"

Kevin shook his head and made a scoop of his lower jaw to accept the bottle once more and took three strong pulls. He heard the empty bottle fall to the floor mat by him. His lips were sticky with the sickly sweet syrup. His vision swam as the stream of warm gel reached his stomach and spread out to engulf him in a toasty blanket of contented ease.

He hadn't gotten high on purple drank since he was a shorty back in Dupont Park. And he sure as shit never drank it straight out the damned bottle like he just did. As he sank back into the enveloping marshmallow comfort he thought of how Nacho would kill him for getting high and falling asleep in the back of his whip. Then he thought of how fall down funny it would be to be killed by a dude named Nacho. Then he dropped lower and lower into fizzy warm bath of inky dark.

7

Gunny Leffertz said:
*"There's a time that's right for you and wrong
for your enemy. You can wait for that time to
happen or make that time happen."*

It was dawn before the party broke up. The sky was
turning from gray to blue, washing the shadows off
the street.

Levon sat in a plastic Adirondack chair on the
screened porch of a house angled across the street
from the split-level that James Tollover bought for
his mama. The house he chose as a hide was boarded up. The door was plastered with foreclosure
notices and sheriff's orders painted over in graffiti.
The porch gave him full view of the front face of
the target house. Close to dawn, a clutch of six men
exited the house for the parked SUVs. They were
laughing and hushing one another and spurred to
louder laughter by the effort to remain quiet.

One of them called out for Mo Dat and the others
shushed him. They got inside their cars. Engines

revved to life. Subwoofers throbbed as sound systems picked up where they left off when the owners parked the night before. They pulled away down MacDougal in a convoy for the next intersection where they turned off in different directions and were gone. The Explorer brought up the rear, its driver unaware of the passenger deeply slumbering in his cargo area.

Only the Cherokee and the Escalade remained where they were. Six gone. That left three inside if Kevin's count was correct.

Levon left the porch to cross the empty street to the split-level. He moved past the Escalade along the driveway and hopped a cyclone curtain fence into the backyard. Using a mini pry bar he popped the lock to the rear door, allowing him into a laundry room.

He pulled the Sig Saur from the holster at his back and parted an accordion door that led into the kitchen. The counters and cabinets were empty except for a microwave and a juicing machine. There was a stack of empty pizza boxes on the table of a dinette set in an eating nook. Empty beer bottles surrounded the stack like sentries. On the floor was a neat pile of cardboard cartons next to a thirty-gallon plastic bin with a drop lid. A water bowl and food dish lay on the tiles by them, both holding easily a gallon in contents.

Of dog food.

Kevin never mentioned the home's other resident.

The squeak of nails on linoleum alerted Levon to the animal's approach. He brought the Sig up in a two-handed grip. A Rottweiler rounded the corner from the dining room. The dog's nails fought for purchase on the slick surface, buying a few seconds of sweet hesitation. There was easily a hand's width between the animal's eyes. Its mouth opened, snout peeling back, to reveal a picket of white teeth set in slavering pink gums. It didn't make a sound as it bounded for him, rear legs bunched for a leap.

The first round took the dog high in the chest but not slowing its momentum. The next two rounds went through the neck and then the skull just below the eye. The rear of the dog's head opened up like a melon spraying the kitchen in blood and matter.

Levon leaped aside, slamming into the door of a refrigerator, allowing the dead animal to crash to the floor in a slide that brought it hard against the front of a dishwasher.

Shouts from deeper in the house. Levon moved at a run for the breakfast nook and out of the enclosing box of the galley kitchen. The dining room beyond had been converted into a weight room with a bench and free weights and an elliptical machine. The voices were closing on him. He dropped low and trained the Sig toward the front entryway with a staircase set on the interior wall and an arched opening beyond.

A figure was hurtling out of that far room, charging up three carpeted steps from a lower level. The sunken living room that Kevin mentioned. A young man in a running suit. Empty hands held out before him and dreadlocks dancing on his head as he came to a stop at the sight of Levon advancing on him. Dreadlocks spun and threw himself back through the archway, tumbling out of sight.

"Shit! Shit!" Dreadlocks shouted.

Levon moved at a run across the entryway. The Sig held before him, the point of the spear.

A metallic clack.

Levon dove to the carpet and rolled back against

a wall.

Peals of thunder broke out from someplace on the other side of the opening. One clap after another. Holes appeared in the walls of the entryway along the staircase. A giant fist punching fissures through three generations of wallpaper and paint. Atomized plaster filled the room with white fog. Buckshot raised splinters from the newel post at the foot of the steps.

From his position at the wall, Levon fired an answering volley of ten rounds in two five-round bursts. Voices from within. One high and shrieking. He thumbed the release sending the empty magazine bouncing over the carpet. He loaded a fresh magazine and rose up to charge the doorway, the handgun held trained forward but tight to his body.

In the sunken living room, a heavy-set man lay on the carpeted floor, holding hands to his calf where blood seeped through the cloth of his pajama pants. The stubby mass of the Keltec shotgun lay, leaking smoke, on the floor by his hand. Dreadlocks was squatting by his fallen homie, fingers reaching for the weapon and eyes locked on the face of the masked white man invading their media room. He pulled his hand back to his side and remained frozen, crouched in a ludicrous impression of a duck.

On a wraparound sofa, a shirtless man in a hoodie turned from the threesome playing out on the big screen. Creamy smoke spilled from the top of an engraved glass bong in his beringed fingers. Hoodie's pupils were the size of dimes and he regarded the scene behind him without full comprehension. A lazy smile creased his face.

"Who invited Die Hard and shit?" he snorted.

8

Gunny Leffertz said:
*"Scare a man and he'll talk. Scare him enough
and he'll tell the truth. But you can only believe
what he says if he believes what you say. He's got
to know you'll hurt him. Truth is something you
both need to share."*

"We ain't gangstas! We thieves!" Dreadlocks, who
turned out to be James "Tolly" Tolliver, kept insisting.

Levon chose the dining-come-weight room for
his interrogation. Tolly was duct-taped onto the
bench of a leg machine. Bread, the heavy-set youth
with the fresh leg wound, was strapped down on the
lifting bench with his leg elevated and tightly bound
with duct tape to stop the bleeding. R.J., the kid in
the hoodie, lay on an exercise mat, bound in a fetal
position with tape around his ankles and wrists. A
thick strip of tape glued his lips together to mute his
nonsequitur remarks and giggling.

"Fucker shot me!" Bread mewled.

"You stole a Mercedes G-Class off the parking

lot at the Iverson Mall," Levon said, ignoring the protestations and complaints.

"Yeah, the fucker shot you, fucker! We ain't gangstas. Shootin' shit up and shit. Shootin' in my house, you dumbass nigga," Tolly said.

Levon realized that the pair were having a conversation and ignoring *him*. *He tore* a strip from the roll of duct tape and slapped it over Bread's mouth.

"You stole a Mercedes G-Class off the parking lot at the Iverson Mall," Levon repeated to Tolly.

"When?" Tolly said, addressing Levon directly for the first time.

"Monday."

"What's this?"

"It's Wednesday morning. It's the car you found the shotgun in."

"Yeah. I remember that one. Found that goddamn shotgun in the back."

"The cops found it that night. Doesn't make sense. You risk stealing a car and just go joyriding for a half hour?"

Tolly grinned.

"I followed one of your crew yesterday. You take the car, drive them a few miles away and dump them. The police find them the same day and have them impounded," Levon said.

"That's our business model," Tolly said.

"How is that a business? How do you make money?"

"The impound garages. They charge the owners for the tow and the holding fees and shit. They pay us a piece out of that. A bounty, yo."

"That pays better than taking them to a chop shop?"

"It's all numbers, yo. Takin' cars to be parted out

means exposure, okay? Interstate transfer and shit like that. Grand theft auto. But nobody asks any questions about joyriders, okay? The cops get to call the owners and say they found their car. Those fuckers are just happy to get their ride back. And the cops get to pretend they're doin' their jobs and shit."

"And the garage cuts you a piece."

"A hundred. More if the ride is extra sweet." Tolly shrugged.

"Which tow outfit pays you?"

"Shit. *Alla them.* Four of 'em have contracts with the county. They work out the territories, who gets what. We call 'em in and drive by once a week for the payday. Like I said, a business model, yo."

"Four garages."

"Biro Brothers. Salucci's. And Knox. And, what's that other fucker's name?" Tolly said, turning his head to Bread who only snuffled and burbled behind his gag.

"Right. Paul Norris. Has a Chevy dealership on Branch," Tolly said, as though prompted by his friend's unintelligible noises.

"Then one of them has the Mercedes," Levon said, tearing a new length from the roll of tape.

"Hold on, yo! Before you do that, what happened to Mr. Jaws?" Tolly said, eyes pleading.

"Mr. Jaws was the dog?"

Tolly nodded, brows wrinkled.

"He's dead."

Tolly blew out a lungful of air.

"Good. That motherfucker scares the shit out of me. Don't wanna be left all tied up with him on the loose." Tolly lifted his face, mouth pressed closed to accept the strip of tape.

9

Levon let himself into the hotel room as quietly as he could. The room was dark, the drapes pulled closed. The TV was on with the volume way down. Merry lay sound asleep in the flickering glow. He picked up the Kindle lying atop the cover by her and touched the screen. The third chapter heading from a book on Thomas Jefferson appeared.

"Good girl," he whispered.

He sat on his own bed and unlaced his boots. He lay atop the covers fully clothed and was out in seconds.

They shared a late breakfast in the hotel restaurant. Levon slipped the waiter a twenty to keep the buffet open an extra twenty minutes. Father and daughter scooped the last of the eggs, home fries, biscuits, gravy and bacon from the chafing trays.

"Can we go to the pool? I'm getting seriously out of shape laying around eating room service," Merry said, wiping her plate with a wedge of toast.

"When I'm done here we'll hit a five star. You can spend a whole day at their pool." He pushed his plate away and filled his cup from a carafe of fresh coffee brought by the grinning waiter.

"That will be when?"

"As soon as I'm done here. Another day or so. Promise."

"Can you bring back some vitamin D then? All these days out of the sun, and all."

He looked up from his coffee to catch her impish grin.

"How about you go for a ride with me?" he said.

Her eyes shot open. She threw down her napkin and shoved her chair back.

"I'll go get my coat," she said as a way of farewell and bolted from the table.

Merry met him in the lobby. It was busy with the arriving and departing. They walked together out to the parking lot. Levon tabbed the key remote and the shiny bronze Escalade roared to a start as they approached.

"Who'd you borrow this from?" Merry asked, eyes askance as he held the passenger door open for her.

"A man named Tolly. He won't need it for a while," Levon said and crossed around to the driver's side while Merry figured out the on-board sound system.

***

"Shit! Shit! What happened? What's this shit?" the voices shouted from the kitchen, out of sight of James Tolliver still firmly taped down on the leg machine.

Took and Nacho came around the corner calling out.

"Tolly! Somebody fucked up your dog, nigga!"

"What's that shit about?"

Both stopped and stared at the scene in the gym room.

"White fucker in a mask. Came in here axing questions," Tolly said when he was freed. He sat in the bench, rubbing his wrists and waiting for the pins and needles in his legs to die down. He sipped a cold two-liter of Dew that Took got him from the refrigerator in the gore spattered kitchen.

"Chuck motherfucker shot me!" Bread whined, wincing as they lifted him to a sitting position. R.J. was up, trailing ribbons of cut tape while looking for his lost bong down in the TV room.

"What kind of questions?" Took said.

"I gots questions myself. Why the fuck is Mo Dat asleep in the back of my fucking Ford?" Nacho said.

"Asshole wanted to know all about our operation. What garages pay us and shit," Tolly said.

"You tell him?" Took asked.

"Of course I fucking told him! He shot Mr. Jaws. He shot Bread! I'm gonna let him shoot me too?"

"This is gonna fuck everything up. You turned in our connections," Nacho growled.

"He ain't interested in our connections, yo. He's lookin' for his car. He's only gonna fuck with *one of them* fuckers. Nobody has to know I told him anything, yo?"

"I need a hospital," Bread said, dropping back onto the bench after an abortive attempt to stand.

"Take a hit of R.J.'s shit and walk it off, nigga. You niggas clean up my mama's house while I take a piss," James Tolliver said and tossed the Dew aside. His legs still asleep, he tested the carpet with the soles of his feet.

"Shit, yo."

All turned to Mo Dat wobbling in the breakfast nook and pointing back to the kitchen with a wavering hand.

"Yo, Tolly, I think your dog is sick, yo."

10

Gunny Leffertz said:
"Being an exterminating son of a bitch doesn't mean you have to be an asshole."

"I don't hear anything," Merry said, aiming the remote at the windscreen and pressing the alarm button with her thumb.

"They'd have disabled the alarm when they stole it. Try the button with the little padlock on it," Levon said.

She tried the lock button as well. No joy.

"We'll try the next place," Levon said and turned the wheel in a U-turn.

He drove along the back fence of Salucci Hauling and Reclamation. An eight-foot hurricane fence topped with loops of razor wire. Sheets of corrugated steel were wired to the fence to hide the contents of the five-acre lot within the enclosure. This was just one of the places in Humboldt County a citizen's stolen vehicle might be towed.

The on-board navigator gave Levon directions

to Paul Norris Chevrolet Kia on Branch Avenue. It turned out to be a big gaudy building of steel and glass. A giant inflatable gorilla stood out near the road before rows of shining sedans and trucks. It held a banner overhead reading: YOU'LL GO APE! The Escalade tooled around the lot, circling the building through the new, used, lease lots and the service area. Merry tabbed the remote but no car alarms sounded. No reassuring bleats from a horn with the pressing of the lock key.

As he pulled back around toward the front he slowed by the dealer's room to allow a car to back into the lane from a parking space. A salesman on a smoke break stepped to the Escalade. Levon rolled the wheel down.

"Nice wheels," he said with a professional smile.

"My wife's. Mine got stolen. We were told to come here to claim it but I don't see a tow lot here," Levon said.

"You drive across the front of the lot and hook a left to the back of the lot. There's a service road there that leads to reclamations," the salesman said, some of the luster of his smile fading.

The service road was paved with crushed gravel that was potted with deep ruts filled with slush. It ended at a large fenced-in lot fronted by a double-wide pre-fab that served as an office next to a big Quonset hut garage housing a pair of tow trucks: a flatbed and a hooked wrecker. The lot was like the others they visited. Eight-foot cyclone fencing. This one had a triple string of barbed wire running around the top strung from Y-shaped stanchions. Strips of faded green plastic were woven through the fence wire to hide the lot's inventory from prying eyes.

Trees grew in close around the back of the fence. There was no road that circled the lot.

Levon and Merry exited the Escalade. They walked past a few parked cars and a waiting taxi toward the pre-fab office.

"Give it a try, honey," he said.

Merry raised the remote and touched the alarm key then the lock key.

A horn sounded from somewhere inside the fence. She touched it again and the horn answered. The short honk was followed by the barking of dogs. Deep, throaty barks. Big dogs. Levon counted three distinct voices. No indication of how many quiet ones, the biters, might be lurking out of sight behind the barrier.

They entered the office building into a waiting room. It had faux-wood paneled walls of an ancient vintage that were decorated with old license plates. A row of steel benches sagged along either wall. The room was a time capsule of '80's tackiness. The floor was grease-stained indoor-outdoor carpeting with a faded groove worn from the door to the reception window. There was even a cigarette machine standing against one wall.

At the end of the room was a reception window fronted by a pane of thick yellowing Plexiglass that appeared to be bulletproof. There was a steel slot at the bottom of the window and all communication was done through an intercom box set by the window.

A large black woman was ahead of Levon in line. She was dressed in a woolen coat over a work smock from a supermarket chain. On her feet were a pair of red galoshes. She was deep in a heated discussion with a sour-looking Asian woman visible behind the glass. Merry stood reading the names of cigarette brands set in a chrome strip across the front of the vending machine.

"Who the hell doesn't take checks?" the black woman was saying.

"We don't. Sorry," said the voice from the speaker. She didn't sound the least bit sorry.

"I'm losing a day of work to be here *and payin'* for a cab *and you're* telling me I can't have my car back?" The black woman enumerated each of her points with a flexed finger ending in a manicured nail of iridescent violet.

"Cash, Visa or Mastercard," the tinny voice said.

"I gotta go to the bank and get cash and come back," the black woman sighed.

"Make sure it's before noon or we have to charge for another day," the voice crackled.

The black woman's shoulders dropped, defeated. Her face deflated.

"Next," the voice said from the speaker.

"This is bullshit," the black woman said and stormed to the door and away, buckles on her galoshes clanking.

"Next," the voice repeated.

Levon stepped to the window. The Asian woman blinked over the top of her glasses and shoved a clipboard with forms atop it through the steel slot at the bottom of the glass. Behind her, Levon could see a cramped office with a pair of metal desks with sheaves of paper in folders piled around computer monitors. A balding white man in shirt sleeves hunted and pecked at a keyboard with supreme indifference. The other desk was occupied by a hatchet-faced man leaning back in a rolling chair and muttering into a phone while picking his teeth with a fingernail.

"What make and model?" squawked the speaker.

"Well, I'll have to come back later. I'm like the lady before me. I thought I could write a check," Levon said.

"Cash, Visa or Mastercard," the tinny voice sighed.

"Sure. What time do you close today?"

"Four-thirty. But if you're not back by noon it's another day, all right?"

Levon looked at the yellowed face of the antiquated Kools clock on the wall of the waiting room. The penguin said it was ten minutes to twelve. He thanked the woman behind the bulletproof screen and, taking Merry's hand, stepped outside.

The black woman from before was by the waiting cab, pacing as she spoke into a cell phone.

"By the time I get to the bank and back here again they'll charge me another two hundred storage *and I have* to pay the cost of the cab *and my supervisor* is going to be pee-ohed at the time I'm losing," she said to the person on the other end, enumerating each point once again with a finger extended from her free hand.

"Miss," Levon said.

The woman turned to him, the phone still at her ear. She eyed him with eyes slitted, no time for any more bullshit.

"What do they want to give you your car back?"

"And what's that to you?"

"Tell me how much."

"They want five hundred and forty-two dollars and eighteen cents. That's if somehow Jesus miracles me the money in the next five minutes. After that even *He has to* pay another two hundred."

"Praise Jesus," Levon said and counted six hundred in fifties and twenties off a roll he took from his jeans pocket.

He held it out to her. She stared at it with mouth agape. She turned her gaze to Merry who was smiling shyly at her. Through the phone at her ear came a tiny metallic voice.

"Who is that? What's he saying to you, Alondra?" the faraway chipmunk voice said.

"Almost noon," Levon said.

Alondra took the money from his hand and rushed over the planks for the office door.

"How are we going to get our car back?" Merry said as they pulled away in the Escalade.

"Another way," Levon said.

11

Gunny Leffertz said:
"There's two things in this world you can't frighten. A hungry dog or an angry woman."

At a Target store he bought ten pounds of ground chuck, a disposable cookie sheet, a quart bottle of ketchup, a couple of boxes of oatmeal, a battery-operated pepper grinder, a carton of Benadryl, a pair of wire snips, and a bottle of Advil PM. The "Fifteen minutes till closing" announcement came over the PA as he pushed the cart to the only open check-out.

"Looks like someone's having a barbecue," the cashier said as she dragged his items over the scanner.

"Yeah," Levon said. He looked away to discourage further conversation.

"Or is it meatballs?" she said and scanned the oatmeal drums.

"Burgers. Five kids. Gotta stretch that paycheck."

"I hear that," she said, placing the last bag on the counter.

***

Headlights out, he drove the Escalade under five miles per hour along the service road behind Paul Morris Chevy. All was dark in the yard except for a light above the office door. The tow trucks squatted in the shadows. A pair of pole lamps illuminated the inside of the impound yard. He pulled into the shadows of some trees growing close to the fence line and cut the engine. The naked strands hanging from an old-growth willow hid the Escalade from view.

Levon got out and dropped the tailgate. Much of the contents of the bottle of Advil PM and a dozen tabs of Benadryl went into the pepper mill. He put on latex gloves and cut a plastic trash bag to lay on the tailgate for a clean work surface. He dumped the whole ten pounds of ground meat on the plastic, upended the open oatmeal containers onto the pile. Next some healthy squirts of Heinz which he worked into the mess with his hands.

He charged the pepper mill to grind the pills down to a fine powder which he emptied onto the heap. The shrill sound of the little motor started some of the dogs inside the fence barking. The baying grew closer then went silent. Through the fence Levon could hear sniffing noses. The barking picked up again.

The meat and other contents were thoroughly mixed and he rolled it into a dozen fat meatballs on the cookie sheet. He stepped up onto the tonneau cover atop the truck bed. From that height he could see over the fence. Below him, on the other side of the fence, four Rottweilers stood on hind legs barking at him. They clawed at the fencing, teeth snapping, eyes aglow with white-hot fury, noses snuffling at the maddening scent of beef blood. The dogs were launching themselves off the packed snow as if to climb the barrier to get at him.

He lobbed the first of the meatballs past them. One turned to sniff. The others kept up their noise, leaping up the fence in an effort to reach the intruder. Levon lobbed another meatball over the barbed wire. This one landed on the ground close behind them. One of them loped over and sniffed once before downing the whole greasy mess in one gulp. The others dropped back off the fence to all fours and went sniffing at the other dog who was now licking its snout with a flashing tongue.

Levon tossed the rest of the meatballs over the fence near them. A brief snarling combat between the dogs broke up when they realized there was enough for all. Within seconds the cookie sheet was empty. The Rottweilers had gotten roughly the same portion of the meatballs so they'd be dosed about the same.

He climbed down and tossed the cookie tray, pepper mill, gloves and the rest of the trash into another plastic can liner, tied it closed and tossed it in the back of the truck. The dogs, finished with their midnight treat, resumed barking and clawing. He shut the tailgate and leaned against it to wait.

The sounds from the other side of the fence grew less enthusiastic. The scrabbling noise died away and the barking turned to indifferent huffs before ending entirely. Levon walked to the fence, gripped the steel grid and gave a few tugs. The grid jingled and rang against the plastic stripping.

Nothing but silence from the yard.

He climbed to the truck bed then onto the roof

of the Escalade's cab. Below him he could see the four attack dogs lying asleep between two aisles of parked cars, chests rising and falling, tongues lolling from open mouths. They would be out for hours. He checked that there was a round in the chamber of the Sig in any case.

After snipping away the strands of barbed wire, Levon threw a leg over the fence and dropped down to the roof of a Miata. He tabbed the remote from the Mercedes. A horn beeped twice. An amber glow blinked near the center of the lot. He dropped to the snow by one of the dozing Rotts. Its nostrils flared in a rumbling snore. The animal was well over a hundred pounds of muscle and teeth. The four of them would have had him down and dismembered in seconds.

He found the Mercedes in a row of cars three in from an intersection of two long aisles of closely packed vehicles. It was unlocked and he squeezed in through a rear door to find the backs of the front seats had been slashed open. The bundles of cash that he'd hidden there were gone. Levon turned on the seat to look in the cargo space. Merry's backpack and his overnight bag were gone as well.

***

Merry was still awake when he got back to their room at the Days Inn. She was laughing at something on the TV. A remains of a salad sat on a room service tray on her bed. She muted the volume and hopped off the bed to give him a hug.

"Looks like you ate healthy for dinner," he said, patting her hair.

"And you smell like burger," she said releasing her

grip on him, her nose wrinkled.

"I'll take a shower before I go to sleep," he said, taking a seat in the occasional chair by the window. On the TV, the show Merry was watching was replaced by a commercial. A broad-shouldered man was mouthing and gesturing before a sun-dappled lot filled with shiny cars. He wore a drooping gun-fighter mustache. His ginger hair was swept back off a high forehead in a mullet that reached the collar of his polo shirt.

"Turn this up," Levon said.

Merry unmuted the TV and the man's voice filled the room.

"—best in new and used Chevrolets anywhere around the Beltway and you have the Paul Norris guarantee on it. You want a deal? You come see the King Kong of the Beltway!"

"That's where we were today," Merry said.

"Bring the family! Free popcorn and Go-Go-Gorillas for kids under twelve!" Paul Norris shouted and waved a stuffed gorilla doll at the camera.

"Yeah. I'll be going back there tomorrow," Levon said, rising from the chair as the commercial ended with Paul Norris high-fiving an actor wearing a gorilla costume.

"Bring me back a gorilla?" Merry said.

"I'll see what kind of deal I can make," he said and walked to the bathroom for a long hot shower.

12

Paul Norris was smaller in person than he appeared to be on television.

On the screen he looked like a retired NFL player. Stepping around his desk to shake Levon's offered hand, he looked more like an accountant.

"Paul Norris. You're looking for a fleet deal?" Norris said, pumping Levon's hand.

"Dave Taylor. I have a contractor outfit up in Gaithersburg. I'm going to need maybe a dozen Silverados," Levon said.

"We can make that happen. Sure we can. What do you have in mind? All-wheel? Eight cylinder? Six?" Norris's broad smile was real. This would be a half-million-plus buy. More if this big redneck could be sold on some goodies.

"Some will be light duty. But a few will be hauling loads."

"Come on out on the floor then. We have a killer media center. We'll go online and see what you like."

"Actually, Paul, I'd rather look at the real thing out on the lot," Levon said.

"You want to kick the tires and smell the leather. I'll get my coat," Norris said, trotting back to his desk for a leather jacket draped over the seatback.

On the way across the show floor they passed a cardboard bin filled with stuffed gorillas.

"Is it okay?" Levon said after plucking one from the top of the pile.

"Sure! You have kids? Take one for each," Norris said, holding the door to the lot open.

"Just the one," Levon said stepping into the cold morning air.

On the truck lot they walked between rows of shiny pickups and SUVs. Norris pointed at various models, touting their reliability and toughness and making sure his new friend Dave Taylor understood that they offered full-service maintenance contracts to all their fleet customers. They came to the end of the aisle where a bronze Escalade was pulled up next to a bank of plowed snow. They were deep along the side lot out of sight of the showroom.

"How would you be financing this, Dave? I ask because—"

"Cash."

The way Dave said it, all the casual bonhomie gone from his voice, made Norris turn to him. The big redneck stood by the Escalade, holding the passenger door open with one hand. In his other hand was a gun. The stuffed gorilla was under his arm.

"Get in."

"Shit. You're from Caskell? What the fuck?"

Levon's eyes narrowed. He raised the Sig. It was trained center mass on Norris who looked more annoyed than scared.

"Get in," he said again.

Norris surrendered and got into the Escalade. Levon tossed the gorilla toy into the back seat and got behind the wheel and pulled off the lot onto Branch heading south.

"Buckle in," Levon said.

"I *paid Caskell*. We're good for now. There's no need for this strongarm shit," Norris said, his tone complaining and bordering on whiny. He buckled in the way he was told to.

"You pulled a Mercedes G-Class off the street two nights ago. It's mine. It had things in it that belonged to me," Levon said as he drove.

"Mercedes?" Norris was having trouble with this new scenario. This Dave guy was not who he thought he was.

"A pile of cash. A child's backpack with Spongebob on it."

"What the fuck are you talking about?" Norris was a good TV pitchman but he was no actor.

Levon said nothing. He made a left off Branch onto a state road continuing south.

"Look, they're going to be looking for me back at the dealership," Norris said.

"You have a deal with a crew of car thieves. They steal people's cars and they let you know where to find them. You charge the owners through the nose to get their own cars back and collect a fee from the county." Levon drove, eyes on the road ahead.

"You want your car back? Let me call the yard. Shit, I'll throw in an oil change and a car wash," Norris said, falling back on his familiar brand of bullshit.

"I want what you took from the Mercedes. I want

it all back."

Norris's face went ruddy. The tip of his tongue played over his lips.

"Where is it?"

"I had to give some of it to the driver and the clerks at the impound office." Norris seemed to shrink in his seat.

"How much?"

"Finder's fee. They split twenty percent."

That would leave just over four hundred thousand.

"And the backpack?"

"Anita wanted it. For her granddaughter."

"Anita?"

"Anita Ho. She works the desk at the impound."

The heartless Asian woman with the immovable noon deadline.

"Where's the money?"

"I don't have it any more," Norris said, chin trembling.

"That's going to be a problem," Levon said, turning the wheel right onto Bryan Point Road where a sign pointed to Piscataway Park.

***

The river flowed past below them, a black stream against the snowy banks. The Potomac swelled with snow melt. Trees stood in the shallows, the water churning against the submerged boles.

The Escalade was alone on a lot situated in the park as a scenic point. Across the river the palatial skyline of Washington rose above the winter-bare trees. The view was wasted on the two men inside the SUV since the windows were fogged over all around.

"I picked all the wrong teams. College football. My picks all sucked ass this year," Paul Norris said, hands knitted together in his lap, eyes cast down as though he were in a confessional.

"Where's my money?" Levon said.

"I'm trying to tell you. I was way behind. I paid off my losses with the money from the Mercedes. I thought it was the answer to a prayer."

"Where is my money?"

"It's gone," Norris said with a petulant shrug. His voice was a whisper.

"It's not gone. Someone has it. Who has it?"

"The Caskells. They do sportsbook out of a piece of shit bar in Dawson. My local guy sold my note to them when I got behind."

"Dawson. Outside Baltimore?"

"Yeah."

"What else are they into?"

"They loan shark. Cigarette smuggling. Anything for a buck. I don't know much else. It's not like we're friends. They said they'd torch my lot, the pricks," Norris said bitterly. The memories still stung.

"What's their organization like?"

"How should I know? Two brothers in a taproom. And some cousin of theirs named Cal. Scary fucker. Looks like a retard with a gym membership. He's the one they send around," Norris said and turned away from Levon, snuffling.

"Give me the address of the bar."

"I don't know the address. It's called Sharkey's. On Kovack near the train tracks." Norris was weeping now, a hand to his face.

"I need one more thing from you then I take you back to your dealership."

"What?" Norris said, turning to his captor, eyes red, snot running into his gunfighter's mustache.

"The backpack," Levon said and tossed a cell phone into his passenger's lap.

13

"I can buy her another one," Paul Norris said, standing on the salt sprinkled front stoop of the duplex in Westphalia. Camille Park, Anita Ho's married daughter, stood in the open doorway with a sweater draped over her shoulders. She invited her mother's boss in but he refused. She looked past him to where a big bronze SUV sat at the curb with the motor running.

"But I like this one!" The shrill voice of a little girl came from somewhere inside.

"You heard her." Camille shrugged. She didn't like Paul Norris. She especially didn't like the creepy smile he was wearing. And she *really didn't* like having him on her front stoop. He'd hit on her a few years back when she came to visit her mom at work once. She was only sixteen.

"Can I at least borrow it?" he wheedled.

"Borrow it? Borrow a kid's backpack?"

"Yeah. Just for a minute." Norris glanced back at the waiting Escalade.

"You're drunk, right?" Camille tugged the sweater more snugly about her and pursed her lips.

"A minute. That's all. Bring it right back." The creepy smile broadened. Norris's brow wrinkled upward in pleading.

"A hundred."

"What?"

"You can borrow it for a hundred dollars," Camille said.

"What the fuck?" Norris's mouth dropped open and his shoulders drooped. This was the final insult.

"You heard me," Camille said and began to close the door.

"Okay! Okay! Shit!" Norris dug for his wallet and counted out tens and twenties that he held out for Camille to snatch away.

She left the door open and went inside. Norris stood on the stoop listening to an argument conducted in a mix of English and Korean and punctuated with mentions of Spongebob Squarepants. The argument rose in volume and tone before stopping short with a child's yelp. Camille returned to the door a minute later and handed the backpack over with a smirk.

"One minute," she said, holding up her wrist to display a watch strapped there. Norris trotted down the walk for the curb.

"Okay!" he called back.

"One second longer and it's another hundred!" she called after him.

Like mother like daughter.

Inside the Escalade, Levon unfolded a clasp knife and cut the seam along the top of the backpack's inner liner.

"Fuck! You didn't tell me you were going to do that! What am I gonna—" Norris stammered. His voice trailed away as he saw the white paper packets spill from inside the lining into Levon's lap.

Levon tipped one of the envelopes open into the palm of his hand. Three diamonds dropped out. Two to three carats, if Norris was any judge. And having been engaged and married three times he was a pretty fair judge.

"One minute!" Camille Park called from the front stoop.

A little girl of about six clung to her leg. She was wearing a new hoodie Levon had bought for Merry at the same time as the backpack. The sweatshirt hung down to the little girl's knees.

"Take it back to her," Levon said, shoving the backpack into Norris's hands.

"But you cut it up," he protested weakly but still he opened the door and climbed out.

The door slammed shut behind Norris as the Escalade leaped from the curb. He stood on the sidewalk, clutching the gashed backpack and watching his ride drive away. He felt a sense of a relief that died in him as suddenly as it had risen.

"One minute. One second," Camille called to him, a hand out to accept more cash.

Paul Norris, the King Kong of the Beltway, threw the backpack to the snow and ran away down the sidewalk.

***

In the men's room of a Subway near an on-ramp for I-95, Levon flushed the SIM card from his cell phone down the toilet. He tossed the rest of the phone into the waste bin.

He pressed SEND on a new phone. Merry picked

up.

"Where are you, Daddy?" she said. Dramatic music filled the background at first before dying away. He pictured her aiming the remote at the television.

"I have to take a little trip but I'll be back by dinnertime. Use this number if you need to call me. We're going to leave tonight. You'll be okay until then?"

"Sure. Where are you going?"

"To a bar."

"You don't drink," she said.

"I'm meeting some people there."

"Do you know them?"

"Not yet."

14

Gunny Leffertz said:
"If you feel like you're being watched you are being watched. If you don't feel like you're being watched, you're being watched by somebody real good at watching."

Cal Shepherd called it The Look-around.

It was that moment when people broke. Either their courage gone, their bluff called, or the delusional protective bubble they called their reality shattered.

It was a shift in the eyes. They looked away from him. Their pupils darted left and right in an involuntary animal reaction. They were looking for a way out when there was no way out.

Sometimes all it took was a talking to. Sometimes breakage. Sometimes a beating. Niggers always took a beating. Irish sometimes. Usually after a fight. Always a short fight since Cal was tree-top tall and wide as a doorway.

He broke the little Jew at the dry cleaners with

pictures.

Cal had the Jew bent down over his own desk, face pressed to stack of receipts. The Jew did The Look-around, eyes searching for a way out. Any way out. Something he could do. Something he could say. Deep in his lizard brain a spark of instinct was fanned to a blaze.

Escape.

But he was pinned by this man mountain who, two minutes earlier, stepped uninvited into his office at the back of the store.

Cal showed the old Jew pictures on a smartphone, scrolling along, showing the Jew pictures of a boy of thirteen climbing out of the back of a mini-van into morning sunshine. The pictures popped up in a time-lapse following the boy as he ran up the front walk of a school building to join other boys and finally enter the school.

"Dad drops him off. Mom picks him up. I have pictures of that, too."

The Jew mewled wordlessly.

"Your grandson is a good looking boy. Joshua? I know guys who like good looking boys like Joshua. Younger the better."

The Jew struggled under Cal's grip.

"You could just have Joshua work off your debt."

The Jew's face was wet with tears.

"Or you could have the twenty thousand here. In full. Tomorrow morning."

The Jew nodded as much as the weight of Cal's arm would allow.

"You know what you did wrong? You got behind with the Caskells. And you have to be the only dumbass in Baltimore who bet the Patriots."

Cal let the Jew up. The man braced himself against the desk to keep from falling. His breath came in long draws, his face flushed red.

Cal walked through the store past rows of plastic-wrapped garments hanging from the conveyor rack. As he stepped around the counter he snagged a fistful of Tootsie-Pops from a cup by the register. He sucked on one as he walked down the block toward the lot where he parked his Sierra.

"Don't bite. Don't bite," he told himself, sucking the sweet cherry candy.

Cal was a biter.

***

Dawson was a close southern suburb of Baltimore. To Levon it looked like more Baltimore, block after block of row homes with doorways that opened onto the sidewalk. Bare dogwoods in sad little squares of dirt at the curbs.

Kovack Avenue ran east-west under the interstate. Driving west toward the CSX tracks, Levon passed through a gentrified area around a hospital. A Starbucks, a florist, a BMW dealership, other boutique stores. Five long blocks along, the street morphed into more bohemian businesses. Another Starbucks, a health food store, used clothing shops, a bookstore, and murals on every available wall. Two more blocks and it was blue-collar residential. Mom and Pop stores or bars at the corners, a lot of them shuttered. Fewer people on the street.

Sharkey's was situated on a corner. Levon almost missed the steel sign hanging over the door. "Sharkey's" in fading script painted over a bilious shamrock. In one window a neon Guinness sign hung before blinds drawn closed. In another window leaned a cardboard sign telling patrons that Sharkey's was closed on Sunday and Mondays. The door was steel with a faux wood facing centered with a pane of bottle-green glass.

Levon drove by slowly. No one on the sidewalk. No cars parked out front. The cross street was a narrow two-lane. He made a right at the next intersection to circle back around where the buildings on Kovack backed onto a nameless alley that ran along the train tracks. Levon went a block east to come back around for another pass by the bar. There was a check-cashing place on the corner opposite Sharkey's. Windows covered by thick bars, the glass piss-yellow from sunshades hanging inside. No street activity there. A day from the middle of the month and payday.

One more turn brought him back to the alley where he made a right to come up the cross street and park the Escalade with two wheels up on the crumbling curb. Other cars were parked the same way despite the no-parking signs posted along the curb.

He walked to the front door with the stubby twelve-gauge under his coat. He cupped the pistol grip in his palm at the hem of the coat. Before entering he closed his eyes tight for thirty seconds. To anyone inside it would appear that he was reading the wrinkled sandwich menu taped to the inside of the glass. It would be dark inside. He wanted to prepare his sight for that.

Inside it was a Pullman car layout. The bar ran down one wall for two-thirds of the building's depth. Beyond it was either an office or a storeroom with access through a door behind the bar. Booths ran down the opposite wall all the way to the back. Levon could see doors for restrooms back there. The smell of decades of stale beer combined with the odor of mustard and cigarette smoke.

The place was empty but for a rail-thin man behind the bar. As Levon entered, the man turned from the television angled on a rack above the rows of amber bottles. On the TV, two women were in a heated argument. The bartender leaned on the bar top, long fingers splayed, sad eyes on the approaching stranger. He said nothing as Levon took a stool before him.

"Is the Guinness on tap?" Levon said.

"Ain't worth a shit otherwise." The bartender shrugged.

"I'll take a pint."

The bartender took his eyes off his customer to take a pint glass from a rack and pull a pint from the tap. Levon shifted the shotgun to his lap, out of sight from behind the bar.

"You have a salt shaker?" Levon asked when the man put the glass before him atop a coaster.

"You really like it that way or are you showing off?" the man said.

"Got a taste for it when I was in the service."

"What branch? I was in the Navy a couple of tours," the man said, turning the volume down on the television with a remote he plucked from the top of the bar.

"I was Navy, too," Levon lied.

"Ship duty mostly. How about you?"

"Same here. Blue water navy all the way from boot to discharge."

"I was on a destroyer. Saw a lot of South Korea and Japan."

"Carriers. I worked flight deck. Persian Gulf," Levon lied further.

"You poor bastard. That's a shit duty," the man said, shaking his head with real sympathy.

"This place seems quiet."

"Regulars start coming in after five. A little bit of a lunch crowd. It picks up weekends."

"Just you?"

The bartender's eyes went to slits. His hands left the bar as he rocked back on his left heel to take a step back from the bar.

Levon raised the shotgun to rest on the leather-padded lip that ran around the bar.

"Let's go meet who else is here," Levon said and nodded toward the closed office door.

Levon kept the stubby Keltec trained on the man while they walked toward the office door with the bar between them. At the end of the bar the man moved his hands to raise a hinged liftgate. Levon slammed the shotgun down atop the liftgate. The man pulled his hands back. Holding the shotgun trained one-handed on the bartender, Levon raised the gate. A stubby revolver was secured to the under-side in a holster. Levon came through the opening, taking the revolver from its place and shoving it in his waistband.

A hand on the back of the man's collar, Levon walked the bartender to the office door marked "private." The bartender entered first, Levon close behind with the shotgun pressed into the man's spine.

A sallow looking man, with a thinning ginger comb-over sat behind a desk, pants around his ankles and his hand working somewhere unseen below the desktop. He looked up, red-faced in outrage from a computer screen that, until seconds before, was absorbing all of his attention. On the screen a man appeared to be forcibly sodomizing a purple-haired Asian woman.

"Pat! Jesus! I thought I told you—" he shouted until his voice died away when he saw the stranger pushing into the office behind his bartender.

Levon shoved the bartender down into a chair facing the desk. He raised the shotgun in his arms to train on the man behind the desk. Behind the man was a wall of piled beer cases. To one side of the desk was an ancient stand-alone safe. Knee-high with a display shelf above it that was crowded with dusty bowling trophies. From the speakers on the computer scream came the sounds of a woman yipping rhythmically.

"Caskell?" he asked.

"One of 'em," the man said, face crimson. His eyes darted past Levon to the open office doorway and back to Levon.

Levon turned his head slightly to look back through the doorway. There was a trap door set in the floor behind the bar. Access to a cellar. He turned back to see the man behind the desk had pulled an automatic from somewhere. Caskell was having trouble gripping it, right hand greasy with lube. He managed a snapshot before Levon emptied a full charge of double-ought into him. The distance between them was under ten feet. The pattern of pellets barely had room to spread. The equivalent of a full magazine of nine-millimeter lead tumbled Caskell back out of his chair. Beer exploded from the wall of punctured cases.

Shoulder checking the bartender to the floor,

Levon strode to the desk and levered the shotgun over the desktop to pump two more rounds into the still-moving body. Blood mixed with beer foam sprayed upwards.

Levon stepped back, pumping another round into the chamber, to find the bartender lying on the floor, hand to his throat. Blood streamed between his fingers in time with his pulse.

Caskell's wild shot has taken out his own man.

Levon was through the door and back into the bar as the hatch in the floor began to lever open. He fired on the walk. Three charges of buck into the floor around the hatch. Splinters flew. The bottles on the shelves jingled against one another while the power of the Keltec's thunder filled the room.

Gunsmoke drifted in the cones of light shining up from below through the ragged holes punched through the floorboards. Levon stood where he was and listened. The streaks of light from below were broken by something moving below.

A series of pops from below. Floorboards split just in front of the toes of Levon's work boots. Plaster sprinkled down on him from rounds striking the ceiling above his head. He raised his elbow to lever the shotgun down at a sharp angle. He pumped his second magazine empty into the floor. Some of the mix in the Keltec's second magazine tube were rifled slugs. Balls of lead the diameter of a pearl onion. They smashed fist-sized holes in the floor.

Levon pulled his Sig and dropped the spent shotgun to the bar. He listened, weapon trained on the cellar hatch. Without shifting his boot soles, he crouched over the holes made in the floor. He sniffed the air. Under the sharp chemical stink of discharged powder other smells rose from below.

The animal stench of blood and feces.

From where he crouched, Levon could reach a rack of glass tumblers. He took one and skidded it over the floor. No sound from below. He skidded another. Nothing.

With the handle of a corn broom he snagged the pull ring set into the hatch and levered the door open a crack. He flipped it up and it rested open on scissor hinges. Moving forward, Sig straight-armed into the dark, pushing the broom handle before him, he pushed the hatch full open.

A man lay down on the concrete floor below the hatch. He was sprawled in the rectangle of watery light reflected off the bottles behind the bar. At least two of the slugs had taken him center mass. He lay frozen where his legs had stopped kicking in the greasy mess of his own carnage. Eyes wide under thick ginger brows.

The other Caskell.

The bartender was unmoving when Levon returned to the office. His fish belly pallor told Levon that he'd bled out during the firefight.

Levon stepped over him for the safe. It was a tough old cast iron job that had probably been there as long as the bar had been open. It was shut tight with the lever at an angle. Levon gripped the lever and pulled it all the way down. Through the polished steel handle he felt the oiled bolts in the door slide free. The door opened with a pull.

Inside were stacks of bills along with sacks of coins. Most of the bills were in the same rubber band wrappers as when they were in the bag in the back of the Mercedes. The rest was in loose stacks or bank wrappers. At first glance there looked to be enough extra to cover the twenty percent share Paul Norris had gifted to his people.

Levon found a beer case in the stack that had not been holed. He dumped the bottles on the floor. Some of them shattered, sending foam over the bare-assed carcass of Caskell Number One. He loaded the bundles of cash into the empty case then wiped the safe's door handle with a tissue from a box on the desk. He exited the office with the box under his arm.

On the way down the bar he retrieved the shotgun. He took the pint glass he'd only sipped from and poured the contents on the floor before placing the glass in the box atop the cash. He scanned the room for anything else he may have touched with his bare hand.

***

"I got just one question," Cal Shepherd said several hours later while he watched the surveillance footage from the camera set over the outside door of E-Z Pay Check Cashing.

"What's that?" said the guy who ran E-Z Pay. Another frightened Jew who watched the screen on which a tall man carried a case of beer to an Escalade parked on Lewis Street. The HD image was crystal clear—clear enough to read the Maryland license plate on the Escalade.

"Why'd he take the broom?"

15

Levon got back to the Days Inn as the early winter dark fell and street lights came on.

"Pack up. We're checking out," was all he needed to say to make Merry leap from the bed and begin jamming clothes into her backpack.

Levon took a shower to wash the residue of Sharkey's from his skin and hair. He changed clothes and put the dirty clothes in a plastic bag to dispose of later.

"Look around. Make sure you didn't leave anything," he said to Merry standing packed, dressed and ready when he emerged from the bathroom.

She did a quick scan of the room, looking under beds and flipping the sheets. She gave him a thumbs-up, anxious to get out of the room she'd called home for past three days.

"All clear," she said.

"Don't forget this," Levon said, producing the stuffed gorilla from his coat pocket.

She smiled and snatched it from his hand.

He left one hundred dollars in twenties for the maid and flipped the doorknob hanger from Do Not

Disturb to Housekeeping Requested. They were in the Escalade and heading south five minutes later.

"Are we stopping anywhere?" Merry asked.

"We need to get some distance. And we need to lose this car." Levon took the ramp for 295 south.

"Can we do drive-through? I didn't have lunch."

"Why not, honey?"

"One more turkey club and I was going to start gobbling."

"We can do drive-through. But only if we eat while we roll. Can you wait until we're another hour out?" Levon said.

Merry suppressed a squeal.

***

The highway rambled west and the view turned to woods and fallow fields as they left the sprawl of the capital behind. The wipers slapped back and forth to smear away the salt spray coming off the road. Traffic was thinning to become mostly trucks.

Merry came alert at each sign for the next exit. She searched the familiar symbols on the following posts for a Wendy's.

"There's a Stuckey's ahead," she said.

"Welcome home to Dixieland," Levon said.

"No Wendy's."

"Maybe next exit."

"Yeah," she said and went silent.

They rode quiet for a while. The radio was tuned to local news/talk and muted. Levon only turned the volume up at the hour and half hour to catch the news. When her father was in this mode, Merry knew better than to play with the dials. He was kind and soft-spoken to her as he always was. Despite that she could sense something in the way he gripped the wheel; the way he sat behind the wheel. Something wound him up tight that only distance would relieve.

She waited until the latest newscast was over to break the silence. Middle East, nuclear weapons, and something a politician said that another politician didn't like. The only local news was college basketball. Her father was still coiled like a spring. Whatever he was listening for wasn't mentioned on the radio.

"Lying is a sin, right?"

"You know it is, honey."

"I feel bad when I lie. But only sometimes. Like I feel bad about lying to those people we knew in Maine. About my name and where we're from and stuff."

"You said you only feel bad sometimes."

"Sometimes I don't. Sometimes lying is fun. Like telling the room service guy how my mom was in the shower and she left me the money to pay him."

"That was fun for you?"

"Like we're spies. Like it's pretend. But it's still a lie. Should I feel bad about thinking it was like pretend?"

"I'm sorry, Merry," Levon said, eyes on the road ahead. "If there's a sinner here it's me. I got us into this and I'm trying to find a way out. I thought becoming new people and getting a new start was the way. I thought you could stay in Maine and be safe and happy. I'm sorry that didn't last."

"It wasn't your fault," Merry said in a small voice.

"That doesn't change things, honey. I did what I did to keep you safe. And there's nothing I wouldn't do to keep you safe."

"Like lying."

"Like lying, honey. And if I have to ask you to lie then I'm sorry about that too. It's all to keep you safe. It's the only way I know."

Merry was quiet for a long while, watching the headlights make a tunnel through the dark. Red taillights described a curve in the road ahead.

"So, it's not the lie but who you tell it to?" she said after a bit.

"That's as good a way of putting it as I can recall," Levon said, turning a second to smile at her.

"Look! Wendy's next exit!" Merry shouted, pointing at the sign flashing past on their right.

16

Gunny Leffertz said:
"Leave a friend behind and you die a little every day. Leave an enemy behind and that fucker might kill you that day."

Mo Dat opened the front door of 6292 West Mc-Dougal to find a super-sized white dude in a leather coat standing on the porch.

"Help you?" Mo said, regarding the Terminator-looking motherfucker through the glass of the storm door.

"Does a James Tolliver live here?" Cal Shepherd asked in return.

"You police?"

"I'm not police. Does he live here or not?"

"Depends on who's axing."

"I'm asking, asshole."

"How's 'fuck you' for a answer?" Mo sneered. He pushed the door closed.

Until the door pushed back. His hand was struck aside with a sudden violent force. The visitor shouldered through the glass storm door, sending a blizzard of shards into the foyer. The edge of the steel-clad door banged into Mo's face, sending him to the floor. Mo's ass struck the spill of broken glass that spread over the floor from the shattered pane. Mo scooted backward over the floor to get away. Glass shards stabbed his hands. He left a bloody smear on the carpet where he bled through the ass of his running pants.

Tolly charged up out of the sunken rec room with a ball bat in his fists. A big white motherfucker stood in the foyer holding a gun on him. Mo was crying like a little bitch at the big man's feet, bloody hands held before him in surrender. Tolly stopped, wide-eyed and tossed the bat aside as if it were electrocuting him.

"I'm looking for James Tolliver," Cal said.

"That's me."

***

"That motherfucker was here! Took my ride!" Tolly insisted to the big man seated at his kitchen table. The dull pewter menace of Cal's handgun rested on the table by the hot sauce spinner. Tolly was making coffee, playing the perfect host. Mo, R.J. and Bread sat at the table opposite. Mo was picking bloody glass bits from the palms of his hands and sniffing back tears.

"You know him?" Cal said.

"Never seen him before. Said we stole his Mercedes. Asked a shitload of questions."

"Shot the dog. Shot me too," Bread said and regretted speaking up when the scary white dude turned to lock eyes with him.

"Questions about what?" Cal said, returning his gaze to Tolly who was setting a steaming mug of black Folgers on the table.

"Our whole damn set-up, yo. The deal we have with the wreckers. All that shit," Tolly said and closed his mouth when the big man raised a hand to him.

Cal sat considering that, working out the connections between a stolen car, the garages that paid bounty on boosted cars and the triple robbery/homicide he left locked up back at Sharkey's. The four men at the table sat holding their breath, all eyes on the scary white dude with the now faraway eyes.

"It was your car he stole?" Cal said at last.

"An Escalade," Tolly said.

"You report it stolen?"

"Hell, no. The papers aren't all in order if you see what I'm sayin'. Good enough to ride around in. Not good enough for the police to be lookin' close at them."

"You have GPS on it?"

"Oh, yeah. It's Lo-jacked."

"Did you contact the service to locate it?"

"I sure as shit did not," Tolly said, shaking his head.

"Why not?"

"'Cause I never want to see that motherfucker again."

"Give me the service and the passcode," Cal said.

"You gonna find my ride?"

"Fuck your ride. I'm looking for the guy who took it."

Tolly got his smartphone from his pocket, accessed the website for his GPS service and entered the passcode.

tollyg0t@$$

Cal made a "gimme" gesture. Tolly sighed and handed the phone over.

"Write down the passcode for me, too," Cal said, tapping the screen where the Escalade was listed on the account of James Tolliver.

"Anything else?" Tolly said as he handed over the slip of paper with the code written on it. Cal took the paper and slipped it into a pocket of his coat along with the phone. He picked up the Taurus off the table. Mo, Bread and R.J. stiffened. Cal stood and replaced the pistol in his waistband at the back.

"Yeah. You need to buy better coffee," Cal said and saw himself out.

***

In the front seat of the Sierra's crew cab, Cal watched the little blue dot moving across the screen of the smartphone. It made a halting progress as the satellite feed corrected its location traveling west on I-66. The Escalade was an hour and a half from Cal's location. More with the shitty traffic around the Beltway at this hour. The tall guy was leaving town with the Caskells' cash.

It was a good lead the tall guy had on him. Didn't matter. As long as he didn't switch cars, Cal could track him anywhere he ran. And for the contents of the safe at Sharkey's, Cal would follow him to California if that's what it took.

With his employers dead, Cal Shepherd looked on that beer case loaded with cash as his severance package.

He put the truck into gear and swung out in traffic to head for the south ramp of 95.

17

It was after nine when Cal Shepherd caught up to the GPS signal from the Escalade. For the past thirty minutes the signal had been stationary near a town in Virginia. New Market. He'd have reached this point sooner but for a jam up getting off the Beltway. Airport traffic.

The ramp off 81 took him to a truck stop. It glowed like a movie set in the dark. The high watt halogens made shimmering novas of light through the haze of freezing rain. There were rows of semis parked on the back lot. A few customers gassed up SUVs and pickups in the glare under the canopy over the pumped stations.

Cal cruised the lot and came upon the bronze Escalade parked at the farthest point of the truck lot. It was streaked white and gray where the rain washed some of the salt rime away. He pulled up a few spaces away from it. He killed the dome light in the Sierra's cab before stepping out with as little noise as possible.

The Escalade was empty. No one seated or sleeping inside. He walked around it twice to check. The hood retained a touch of engine heat at the center. The doors were locked. Through the tinted glass of the rear windows he could see something lying on the cargo bed. A canvas bag of some kind. Didn't look big enough to hold the cash from Sharkey's. No broom. No beer case. He should have taken an extra remote from the niggers back on McDougal. Sure thing they had another set of keys.

No problem. He'd come back once he found his man and break into the Escalade if he had to.

He drew his collar up and hiked to the truck stop. The MyWay HiWay. Cute.

He stood under the eaves out of the rain and feigned interest in the movie selection posted on the front of the Redbox vendor. The interior of the place was brightly lit and he could see patrons seated in booths and waiting at the counters. The shelves of snacks, souvenirs, auto supplies, and T-shirts were high and created blind spots he couldn't see around.

Cal killed as much time as he could at the Redbox and didn't spot the tall man he'd seen so clearly exiting Sharkey's five hours earlier. Some trucker with a chain wallet and Viking beard cleared his throat behind Cal.

"Don't see anything I like," Cal said and moved away from the DVD dispenser to the side door of the truck stop.

The place was muggy warm inside. The air was thick with the smell of coffee and pork grease. Cal walked the aisles and scanned the clientele. No tall guy. He stepped back to the restroom area and entered the men's room. He took his time at a urinal until everyone had done their business and the stalls emptied out. On the way out he glanced into a room off the side of the lavatory where a row of shower stalls stood against a wall. No luck.

Cal snagged a large black coffee and a Tootsie Pop before crossing the lot back to the Sierra. The Escalade was still in the spot where he'd left it. He sat a while in the Sierra, sipping coffee and watching the lot behind him in the rearview. People came and went but no one walked toward the back lot.

Shrugging out of the cab, he reached into a side pocket of the door and retrieved a ballpeen hammer. Cal waited until the lot was empty before breaking in the driver's side window. He used the sleeve of his leather coat to clear the beads of glass from around the frame.

Inside the Escalade, he pulled the tab to pop the back window and slid out to go to the rear of the SUV. He reached in the open hatch and pulled the canvas bag there toward him. Inside was a shotgun of some kind. It looked like something out of a space movie. Would the guy leave this behind? Cal worked the pump. The action clacked empty. He tossed the Keltec back into the cargo area and drew the canvas bag over it.

He looked inside the cab on the seats and on the floor. Nothing else but a single discarded wrapper from Wendy's.

Cal sat in the warm interior of the Sierra, sucking on the candy pop.

Did the guy leave the Escalade and steal another car? Not likely. He was gone thirty minutes or more. Plenty of time for someone to notice their ride was gone. Maybe he hitched a ride with a trucker. That made no sense. The man's got cash on him, cash out the asshole. A taxi? No way. No taxis in this bumfuck speedbump of a town.

Or maybe he walked away. Took the cash and walked into New Market. Sleepy little hayseed town was a better place to boost another car.

Cal put the truck in gear and made a left out of the lot, following the signs that told him that New Market was only one point five miles to the east. He drove easy, wipers snicking frozen pellets away, his headlights bouncing dancing spots of light off the slick road surface. He eyed the shoulder of the road for pedestrians.

"Don't bite, don't bite," he said to himself in time with the wipers.

18

Gunny Leffertz said:
"Sometimes it's hard to tell where the battle-field ends or when the war is over."

The Trailways bus stop in New Market was at the Dogwood Grill on Main. The bus down to Nashville, Tennessee would stop there around eleven, four nights a week, so long as someone at the Dogwood called the Trailways office and told them there were passengers waiting. There were no tickets sold at the counter. Passengers paid the driver when they boarded.

That suited Levon just fine. The driver would take cash and wouldn't do more than glance at his driver's license with his photo and the name Mitch Roeder.

He sat in a booth facing the front door with Merry seated across from him. The one wall of the Dogwood was booths across from a long counter with twelve stools lined along it. A few locals were seated. A senior citizen couple in another booth behind Levon. A young college-aged kid absorbed in a laptop sat in a booth closer to the door. Two sheriff's deputies took up a pair of the stools and were bantering with a man in a stained apron who was working the grill and register on his own. Country-pop played softly from a radio on a shelf on the wall behind the counter.

Levon had coffee and Merry drank a hot chocolate. She held her hands cupped to the sides of the steaming mug. They needed the hot drinks to take the chill off after the cold walk into town from the truck stop. The freezing drizzle turned to a steady rain as they walked along the shoulder to where the town's sidewalks began. Now it was a downpour that hammered against the big pane of glass at the front of the place.

The canvas bag of cash rested on the floor under the table. Merry had her new backpack and her father's new overnight bag on the bench seat beside her.

"You warm enough, honey?" Levon asked.

"Starting to be." She smiled through the sweet steam rising from the mug.

"The bus'll be here soon. Another hour or so. You need to change out of those wet clothes?"

"I'd sure like to put on dry socks and jeans."

"Finish your cocoa and I'll walk you back," he said.

"Daddy, I'm going to be twelve in August," she explained.

"And this is a strange town and you're still my little girl."

Merry pulled her backpack off the bench and started for the back. Levon walked behind her to the restrooms set against a side wall at the rear of the grill. The two doors, marked GUYS and GALS were set to one side of a corridor leading to a rear exit door. The other side of the corridor was a locked storeroom. The rear door was steel clad with a panic bar. A sticker on the door warned that a fire alarm would sound if the door was opened.

"See? No perverts or ninjas or grizzly bears," Merry said holding the door to the ladies room open for her father's inspection. It was a single occupancy with a toilet and basin.

"The plural for ninja is ninja," he said.

"Homeschool dads," she laughed as she closed and locked the door behind her.

Levon returned to the booth and sat sipping coffee. He kept the deputies in his peripheral without ever looking at them directly. They were speaking to one another in low voices with an occasional interjection from the counterman. This was a nightly ritual. The three men knew one another well, were easy around each other. Probably all grew up in this town or nearby.

An older couple scooted out of a booth behind Levon and made their way to the register up front where the counterman rang them up while exchanging some small talk. He cautioned them to stay dry and they assured him that they would as they exited. A tiny brass bell hung over the top of the door tinkled softly over the hiss of rain striking the sidewalk outside.

The bell sounded again a few moments later. A man in a leather coat stepped in from the dark. His coat was running with rainwater. Well over six feet with the broad shoulders of a linebacker; a linebacker gone to seed with a paunch belling out the corded sweater he wore under the coat. The man stood a moment, scanning the restaurant with his eyes, never turning his head. His gaze rested on the deputies who were listening to a story being told by the counterman. Neither of them turned to check out the new arrival. The big man's eyes arrowed for a beat as they passed over Levon. He hesitated for a fraction of a second before stepping over to take the seat at the end of the counter nearest the register.

Levon watched the big man. He caught a glance from the man until the other man turned his head forward. The counterman concluded his story to the amusement of the deputies and moved down to the end to take the new customer's coffee order. The counterman came back with a mug and menu for the man on the end stool before returning to the deputies.

Waiting until the three men were once more involved in their conversation, Levon rose from the booth. He glanced to the back of the place. Merry was still inside the ladies room. She'd be in there a while longer. The big man at the counter did not turn as Levon moved behind him. He could sense that the man's full attention was on him in any case. Levon moved past the man's orbit. His boot soles squeaked on the rain slick linoleum. The bell tinkled as he stepped through the door to the sidewalk.

He stood under the awning before the grill a moment. He hunched his shoulders in the soft light coming from within before turning right to walk down the street in the driving rain.

Levon walked along the dark storefronts that lined the empty sidewalk, willing the big man to follow.

19

Gunny Leffertz said:
*"Trouble will always find you. So pick the
ground and hang on."*

He was made. He knew it.

Cal stirred the coffee with a spoon for something
to do. The asshole brought him a spoon even though
he'd ordered black.

Cal weighed his options. He shrank them down to
one. The tall guy—and Cal's shot at the money—was
walking away.

The cops were bullshitting with the asshole behind the counter. They didn't even turn when Cal
tossed a five to the counter and made for the door,
leaving the coffee still swirling in his mug.

The street was dark. The rain beat down on him.
The field of white noise drowned out everything as it
fell on cars pulled into the curb. It drummed off store
awnings and pelted the sidewalk. The street was
empty in either direction. The street lights blinked
yellow at the intersection. One-horse, broke-dick,

redneck town. The storefronts were black mirrors in which he could see his reflection flickering on rain-streaked glass. The only lights came from the Dogwood Grill and a drug store on the corner across the street. No one on the sidewalk.

Cal sped his pace to a trot. He bent to look for shadows inside any of the cars parked along the curb. He passed a Volvo mini-van, a POS Chevy pickup and the sheriff's cruiser. No one inside. The sidewalk clear. No way in hell the tall man made the corner ahead of him.

"Who sent you?"

The voice came from the well of a storefront. A florist. Cal turned on a heel. His eyes found the black shape in the shadows of the recessed entrance, lined either side by display windows. Six steps separated them. Cal stood in the rain, hands out from his sides. The Taurus out of reach for now.

"Nobody sent me. Nobody's left."

The man in the shadows said nothing. Cal blinked rainwater out of his eyes, watching the guy's outline. He couldn't see the man's hands.

"Tell me where the money is and walk away," Cal said.

"Baltimore. The bar."

"Yeah. I worked for those guys. Now I'm looking after their business interests."

"That money is mine. You're the one who's going to walk away," the guy said. His voice was even and without inflection.

"I didn't come here to deal, dickhead," Cal said, leaning forward as though to hear the guy better over the rain. He calculated the distance between them. He shifted a foot back on the slick sidewalk, placing his weight forward.

"Neither did I," the guy said.

Cal launched.

***

Levon let the big man close with him. The weight of the big man slammed Levon back against the front door of the florist shop. The glass starred but held. The big man's hands were on him. Levon blocked one hand with his left arm, levering it away. The second hand found his throat. The fingers wrapped around his neck, the thumb pressed hard against his windpipe. The glass crackled and splintered against the back of his jacket.

The Sig in Levon's gloved fist was pressed tight between them.

He pulled the trigger once. Twice.

The sound was muffled by the bulk of the big man. The force of the two shots caused the big man to lean away, his fingers releasing their grip on Levon's throat.

Levon got a handful of the man's coat and pulled him close once again. The big man clawed for Levon's face even as his legs sagged beneath him. Levon pulled hard to keep the man upright in a wobbling embrace.

With the handgun crushed between them once more he fired three more rounds. The discharges echoed in the recessed storefront like polite coughs.

The big man went limp and Levon relaxed his grip. The big man dropped to the tiled floor of the entryway. Levon replaced the Sig in his waistband. He could feel the warmth of it radiating through his shirttail.

Levon crouched over him, going through pockets of his pants and coat. A ring of keys and a key remote with GMC stamped on it. A wallet, a money clip with a thick bundle of bills, a snub-nosed Taurus in a clamshell holster at the small of his back. Levon stuck all of these in the pockets of his coat. He took a Breitling watch from the man's wrist and slid it onto his own. He then hefted the man under the arms and dragged him as far into the shadows of the storefront as he could. The rain and the dark would hide the corpse until morning.

He searched the ground for the five spent shell casings and pocketed those as well before stepping from under the store awning into the freezing rain.

The blood of the big man was all over him. Levon stood on the sidewalk, face up and arms held wide. He let the rain soak his clothes. It would wash the worst of the blood away. To anyone who might have seen him he would look like a drunk imploring Heaven for guidance. He pulled a glove off with his teeth and wiped a damp hand over his face.

***

Merry had taken his seat in the booth. She sat white-faced, eyes on him as he reentered the Dogwood Grill.

"You look like you been swimming, buddy," the counterman said.

"Had a smoke. Those cigarettes are a bitch," Levon said in return, gesturing with a thumb, face turned away.

"Nasty habit. Glad I quit last year," one of the deputies said. The men went back to their conversation. The kid at the laptop never looked up.

"Grab up your stuff, honey. Time to go," Levon

said to Merry.

"Is the bus here?" she asked, a quaver in her voice.

"We're not taking the bus. Your Uncle Fern called me on the cell. He's coming by to pick us up."

"Uncle Fern."

"Right."

Levon dropped bills on the table. He hefted the canvas bag and the overnight. Merry slipped her arms into the backpack straps.

The counterman thanked them and Levon waved without turning, holding the door open for Merry to step outside.

"You have blood on your face and your neck," Merry said as they walked down the sidewalk.

"None of it's mine," Levon said. He stabbed out with the key remote, depressing the lock pad. He got no response until they reached the corner. The muted bleat of a car horn came from somewhere out of sight.

A forest green Sierra sat parked on the empty lot next to a bank halfway down the intersecting street. The running lights flashed yellow. Levon unlocked it. Merry climbed in the passenger side while Levon heaved their bags into the back seat of the crew cab. Merry hugged her arms tightly about herself. Her chin quivered. He started the truck up and turned the heater on full blast to let her warm up a bit. Then he pulled onto the street and made a left.

On the way back to the highway he drove slowly past the Dogwood Grill. The county sheriff's cruiser was gone from where it was parked. Only a minivan and a beater pickup truck remained at the curb. Levon peered into the black mouth of the florist's entryway but could see nothing but shadow.

They were on the highway an hour before Merry spoke. The car was muggy warm. Levon dialed the heat down, cutting the fan from a roar to a murmur.

"I came out of the bathroom and you were gone."

"I'm sorry, honey. I really am."

"You smell. What's that smell?"

He didn't answer. He couldn't think of what to tell her.

"It's the blood, isn't it?" she said, voice small.

He only nodded.

"Can we pull over?"

He pulled the truck to the shoulder. Merry unbelted and opened her door to vomit. He unbelted to move closer to her, to put a hand to her back. Her shoulders heaved. She spat.

"It's all right. It's nerves, is all," he cooed to her, his voice a whisper.

He found tissues in the center console and offered her some to wipe her mouth.

"We'll ride with the windows down until I can get out of these clothes, all right?"

She nodded, the wad of tissues to her mouth. The color was back in her cheeks.

Windows down, cold clean air buffeting them, they drove on west into the night.

"Where are we going? When will we stop?" Merry asked.

There was a plaintive tone there he'd never heard before. She was hurting. She was afraid. There was no way she could know where he went when he left their booth. There was no way he could make her understand or make it right. Except that, in her mind, she imagined a hundred scenarios, a hundred reasons why he might be gone. In very few of them did she imagine him coming back. Ever. And now, here in the truck cab with the stink of another man's blood filling the air, those imagined terrors were made real.

"We're going some place where you can feel safe. And we're not stopping till we get there," Levon said.

20

There was a bite in the air still. Mississippi winters were generally mild but for a few days late in the season. The locals referred to it as the sting on the tail, old man winter's last hurrah. Well, the old bastard had hurrahed himself hoarse this year. There was frost on the trees and even some snow still unthawed in the shadow of the birch woods.

But the sun was warm and that was what Gunny Leffertz enjoyed most about the walks with Joyce. He turned his face up to let the rays touch his skin. He couldn't see the light but he could feel it. The radiance cut through the chill. He took in a deep breath through his nose. It still smelled like winter to him. But give it a few weeks and he'd be able to smell the green sprouting all around. The woods, silent now, would fill with the thrum of flying bugs. The stream that ran alongside the mile-long driveway would be thawed, its lazy current chuckling around the rocks. The swish of wind through the leaves would be all around.

For now, the only sound he could hear was the

rubber soles of Joyce's wellies crunching on the hard-packed gravel.

"Sun feels good," he said.

"It does," Joyce agreed.

She walked close but did not take his arm or offer any other aid but her company. The old jarhead resisted any kind of help on these walks. And as an old jarhead herself, Joyce understood Gunny's need to take these walks without help from her. He knew every inch of the way of the long driveway that led from the road to the cabin he shared with his wife. Gunny walked it easy at a normal, steady pace. No one who did not know him would suspect he was stone blind, his eyesight lost to a tiny sliver of Russian steel in Iraq in '91.

Most of the year these walks down to the mail box were just a part of the daily ritual. The box was usually empty except for a few pieces of junk mail. Gunny and Joyce's pensions from their days in the Corps were direct deposited and neither of them had any family they ever heard from.

Closer to spring though, the walks to the box took on a note of anticipation. Joyce, an avid gardener, looked forward each year to the new catalogs from the seed companies. She'd read them aloud to Gunny, noting each new addition or offering. He'd sit with a mug of coffee and listen to the sound of her voice, infused with a childlike excitement, as she planned the garden she'd plant when the ground was warmer. He'd help as much as he could, turning over the earth or watering or hauling sacks of manure. Joyce did most of the work but that was her joy. His joy was in sharing her happiness. And all those fresh grown vegetables, of course.

He felt the ground slope more sharply beneath his

boot soles and knew they were coming to where the drive met the unpaved township road. Gunny stood by while Joyce went to the box, a faded red steel rural box decorated both sides with the Marine eagle, globe and anchor. He heard the squeal of the door opening followed by the click of it latching back in place.

"Something addressed to you," she said, returning to where he stood.

"Who from, my dear?" he asked and held out his hands. He felt the cardboard box she placed in his hands. It was roughly the size of a shoebox and sealed with slick tape.

"There's no return address. It's posted with stamps," she said.

"What kind of stamps?"

"Battle of New Orleans and Janis Joplin."

"They gave Janis her own stamp?"

"Looks like, Gunny."

He tucked the box under his arm and turned back to the house. Joyce walked alongside, new catalogs from Burpee and Smith & Hawken rolled up in her hand.

At the house, Gunny set the box on the kitchen table. He took his clasp knife from his pocket and severed the tape to open the box. A second box rested inside, set in a nest of bubble wrap.

"What is it?" Gunny asked, holding up the slick laminated box he found inside.

Joyce took the box from his hands.

"It's a satellite phone. With a recharger station. There's no note or receipt or anything. What does it mean?"

"It means we're going to have company soon," Gunny said.

TAKE A SNEAK-PEEK AT BOOK FOUR: LEVON'S RUN

Book four of the relentless Levon Cade series is full of unforgiving action.

The FBI, ATF, Homeland Security and police departments from seven states are on the trail of Levon Cade and his daughter Merry. Man-killer Levon leads his pursuers into the heartland where he means to lose them forever. But his plan turns into a desperate fight for survival as he enters the shadowy world of human traffickers.

Heaven help any man who stands in the way of Levon's run.

"Levon is bad ass. Makes Jack Reacher seem like a crossing guard."

COMING FEBRUARY 2022

1

Bando blamed his bitch of a girlfriend for everything.

If his bitch of a girlfriend didn't spend all the money he gave her for their kid.

If his bitch of a girlfriend didn't keep bitching about visiting her mother in Miami. Bitched that Connecticut in February was too damn cold. Only she didn't have any money because she spent every dime he gave her for the kid.

If his bitch of girlfriend could just learn to budget he wouldn't have had to rob that Xtra Mart.

If he hadn't used her car to rob the Xtra Mart.

If the bitch hadn't told the cops he borrowed the car.

If the bitch didn't tell them where to find him.

It was all his bitch of girlfriend's fault that he was locked up in Middletown City Jail, a guest of the county.

Only good part of all of it was that the cops got all the money.

His bitch of a girlfriend wouldn't be visiting her mother in Miami.

2

"Notice something about these bills?" said the guy from Westbrook Barracks.

"They counterfeit? We thought they might be fake. You never see anything bigger than a twenty at a place like that," said the Middlesex County deputy. He leaned over to look at the bill held stretched between the gloved hands of the trooper.

"They're old," the trooper said.

"Look new to me," the deputy said.

The county had called in Connecticut State Police CID when they spotted the bills taken in as evidence in a convenience store hold-up. They found Lyle James Bandeaux high as a kite in his apartment just as his girlfriend said he'd be. The money was still in the Xtra Mart bag. The weapon used in the robbery was on the floor by him. Dead bang.

"That's the other thing. Series 1993 but still fresh. They're old but they look new." The trooper flicked the edge of the bill. It was crisp.

"Damn," the deputy said, squinting at General Grant's stern visage.

***

Connecticut State CID contacted the Federal Reserve Bank in Boston. The trooper faxed over scans of both sides of both bills. The scans remained on the fax machine tray at the Fed until the following morning. An officer there re-faxed the notice from the trooper to Treasury and the FBI.

Old money, especially old money that is clearly uncirculated, makes Fed Reserve officers put down their coffee mugs, sit up, and take notice. The Fed runs a tight ship. An even tighter ship after millions in bills vanished from the reserve bank in Philadelphia back in the 1970s. Used, torn, soiled or simply filthy currency winds up at the Fed for disposal. Before the thefts, the bills were counted and then incinerated. The systems had holes. Lots of holes. And it didn't take a mastermind to hold a few bills back from the fire and slip them into a pocket. It was an inside job that went on for years; a slow-motion looting of old currency slated to be destroyed; a conspiracy of otherwise honest bean counters who couldn't resist the temptation of slipping away with a few dirty old bills that no one would miss. A few dirty old bills turned into wads and wads of dirty old bills adding up to millions.

The thefts were discovered and the Fed was turned upside down and backwards. Officials were fired. Employees went to jail. A few committed suicide. An embarrassment and a tragedy.

The Fed's entire security protocol was then altered to account for every single bill entering the system. Bills to be destroyed are stamped through by a die upon arrival at the bank. The shape of the die identifies which of the twelve reserve banks has taken in each bill. The money is scanned, counted, re-counted, shredded, bleached and spun to a consistency of cotton candy after which it is bagged, tagged and stored in the depths of each Fed branch. At every step of the way, there are more cameras on all involved than at a celebrity wedding.

Long story short, every bill is important to the Fed. And when a pair of fifties, twenty plus years old, and so mint that the ink still stands raised on the rag stock, the Fed gets curious about where those Grants have been all this time and where they came from.

FBI special agent Bill Marquez thought he knew.

3

Bill needed a decent meal, a long hot shower and twelve hours sleep. He wasn't going to get any of it.

He was attached to an ongoing investigation into a home invasion in the woods of Maine. It was part of a string of violent invasions that occurred over the past month or so ranging from Costa Rica to Thailand to Fiji. The crew involved was on the hunt for a big boodle of cash stolen years before by billionaire conman Corey Blanco. They tortured and murdered Blanco and his wife and kids. Then the same crew went on to systematically burglarize other Blanco properties around the world. They left corpses behind everywhere they went.

The latest happened a little more than twenty-four hours before in a flyspeck town in Maine. There were dead victims scattered everywhere around a lake community. There were terrorized survivors, including a kid in a Bangor hospital getting some fingers sewn back on.

Most of the invasion crew were dead. Six, possibly seven, of the actors died at the hand of someone unknown. Shot, stabbed, and in one case, beaten to death. Witnesses gave up nothing on how any of it went down. They pleaded ignorance or refused to cooperate. Early theories were put forth that the gang turned on each other. They found what they were looking for then went blood simple and began taking one another out until they were all dead. An ouroboros serpent of greed.

Based upon the evidence on the ground around Lake Bellevue, Bill Marquez had another idea.

This gang had never left witnesses at their other break-ins. Up in Maine they killed three innocents but left a woman, her daughter and her son alive. On the prior robberies, millions in cash and valuables were left behind. The operating theory was that these guys were pros searching for a particular item. They were so slick they left behind any loot that might later lead to them. This time there were signs that cash and jewels were taken.

And there was the last man standing. Or, more precisely, driving.

Someone survived the slaughter and made it through the woods to take off in one of two getaway cars stashed on a fire road miles from the primary crime scene.

And then there were the three lake residents unaccounted for. Two were a man and his daughter with identities that proved to be bogus. The man left his truck behind but he and the little girl were nowhere to be found. The cabin they shared showed signs of a break-in but no signs of violence. Then there was a woman, also using a phony name, illegally squatting in a mansion directly opposite the Blanco home. The owners of the house were contacted at their winter residence in the Bahamas. They never heard of their uninvited house guest and had not given anyone permission to stay there. The mystery woman's Mercedes G was gone as well.

Now Bill was sitting in the cramped and stuffy manager's office in the back of an Xtra Mart in New Haven. He was reviewing surveillance video on a pair of monitors. One showed the gas pump island. The other offered a view of the store's counter. The manager was a nervous Egyptian guy eager to help. He leaned over Bill's shoulder, breathing garlic in his ear.

"Your sign says you don't take bills larger than a twenty," Bill said as he moved the mouse to race backward through the footage showing the customers at the counter.

"My cousin Yuri is an idiot. He took the money. I tell him and tell him," the manager groused.

"Why did he take it?"

"I told you. He is an idiot."

"Maybe the guy let him keep the change," Bill offered.

The manager huffed a fresh gust of garlic.

On the monitor, Bill watched the high-speed reverse pantomime of Lyle James Bandeaux holding a gun on the counter man and fleeing the store, a plastic bag containing the contents of the till in hand.

"It would be just before that." The manager waggled a finger at the screen.

"How can you know? You watch this?" Bill said without turning from the whirl of customers gliding up and away from the counter in fast-backwards time.

"We do safe drops every hour. The two bills you

are looking for were still in the register."

Bill shrugged.

"There!" The manager stabbed at the screen.

Bill froze the image.

A big guy, broad shoulders, stood at the counter. Ball cap with a hoodie worn under a heavier winter coat. The hood was up over the ball cap. The man's face, even the shape of his head was concealed. Facial recognition programs were going to be useless. His nose, upper lip and chin were visible. He had a week's growth of facial hair. He was a white guy. Despite a clear HD image that's all the video revealed.

Bill wound back and watched the exchange play out from the start in real time. The guy entered to take a place in line behind a pair of young black teens buying sodas. Once they left, he stepped to the counter. He handed over two bills in a gloved hand. There was an exchange between the man and Yuri, the manager's idiot cousin. The cousin gestured with open hands, head shaking. The customer remained unmoving, hand held out with the two bills stiff between his fingers. Yuri gave in at last and took the bills. The guy turned for the door and left.

"Wait." The manager placed a hand atop Bill's hand working the mouse.

Together they watched Yuri ring up the sale, place the two bills beneath the register drawer. Before closing the drawer, he slipped a couple of bills from the tray and pocketed them.

"Son of a bitch!" the manager hissed, releasing Bill's hand.

Bill checked the time stamp on the video. Less than nine hours ago. He switched to the outside footage and moved back to the same time. He watched the hooded man walk to a Mercedes SUV parked by the gas pump island. The same model as the Mercedes that was missing from Lake Bellevue. The man stood pumping gas. There was someone seated inside the SUV in the passenger seat.

"Does this have a zoom feature?" Bill asked.

The manager pointed to a magnifying glass symbol in a drop-down toolbox atop the screen. Bill moved the cursor to the face visible through the windshield and dialed in. A female face. Shoulder length hair. The image was blurred but Bill could see it was a young girl. The mystery man's daughter, if she was his daughter. The angle didn't allow him to see if there was anyone in the back seat.

He watched the man pump the gas, re-hook the nozzle, re-enter the SUV and drive off frame. Then he wound it back and zoomed in on the license plate. Massachusetts plate. He copied the plate numbers on a slip of paper.

Bill asked the manager to make a disc copy of the footage for him. While he waited for the disc to burn he called the FBI office in Boston. He didn't know anyone there. He'd been assigned to the LA office for the past few years. He put on his "take no shit" voice until he got through to an assistant director of that division.

The manager handed off the disc, still warm from the burner. Bill's cell rang back.

"Marquez."

"We ran that plate. The Mercedes is registered to a Kiera Anne Reeves. Listed residence in Boston."

"Can you get someone over there to lock her down? She's a person of interest in this Lake Bellevue mess."

"We won't have to. Cops in Waltham, Mass have her in custody."

Bill peppered the Boston AD with questions as he ran from the store to his car, the disc in hand.

4

"I'm the victim here. Can we try to remember that?" Kiera Anne said.

"What were you doing in that motel room?" Bill Marquez said. His eyes felt like they were filled with sand. The drive back up to Boston hadn't helped.

"I was on vacation," Kiera Anne said, eyes level across the table in the interrogation room. She lowered her head to speak directly to Bill's smartphone set to record the interview. He noticed a bruise on her chin that she'd tried to cover with makeup. In the harsh overhead light, it took on a yellowish hue.

"The room was registered to a Noah Murray of Galveston, Texas."

"Good old Tex," she sighed.

"In addition to playing rough, good old Tex doesn't exist. Why are you protecting someone who left you duct-taped on the bed for the maid to find?"

"I met a guy in a bar. He took me to his motel. Is that a crime?"

"Motel 6 seems kind of down market for you."

"I like an adventure now and then," she said, covering the Patek Phillipe watch on her left wrist with her right hand. She shook her head to free a strand of blonde hair from over her eye and regarded him with a flat expression.

"Let me tell you what we have, okay? Lay my cards on the table and see if you can explain my hand," Bill said, voice as flat as her gaze.

She shrugged and sat back in her chair, eyes closed and mouth downturned.

"We found you trussed like a Christmas present on a bed in a motel room paid for in suspect cash and registered in the name of a man who never was. We also found a Suburban with Canadian plates parked on the lot. It was rented in Toronto under the same stolen name and account as another Suburban found at the scene of a mass murder up in Maine. And your car, a Mercedes G class, was caught on video at a convenience store down in New Haven driven by an unidentified man in the company of a female minor."

"I told the police here it was stolen," she said. There was a pack of cigarettes on the table. She reached for it and peeled away the cellophane.

He glanced at the sign on the wall that read, This Is A Non-Smoking Facility.

"Do you mind?" she said, eyebrow arched.

Bill shrugged and hit the switch by the door, turning on a room vent. He lit the cigarette for her. She released a blue cloud to the ceiling. She cleared her throat and stifled a cough. Not a regular smoker. She was looking for a distraction for herself. For him.

Her hands were steady, he gave her that. But there was a dew of sweat on her upper lip. Her eyes caught him studying her.

"I saw the report on your car. But that's Waltham

P.D.'s problem. The bureau doesn't do auto theft. Would you like to tell me what you were doing in Maine?" he said, retaking his seat across from her.

"Who said I was in Maine?" She flicked ash onto the floor, elbow cupped in her hand, acting casual as hell.

"Because that's what fits. You were married to Courtland Ray Blanco for five years. Divorced fourteen years ago. We have witnesses placing you in Bellevue, Maine for the past month." That was a lie. The three witnesses they had were giving them squat for now. "Your ex-husband was the target of a gang of international thieves who were working their way around the world burglarizing homes owned by him through holding companies and shell accounts. You just happened to be trespassing in a home with a view of Blanco's house on Lake Bellevue at the same time as that home was invaded."

"And you have proof of that," she said.

"Fingerprints. DNA. Everything you see on TV." Another lie. A white one. He expected a report from the crime scene techs confirming her presence in the house. He suspected she cleaned up after herself but, after weeks in that house, she was bound to have missed something.

"You're arresting me for staying in a house that isn't mine?"

"Criminal trespass is a local cop thing. I'm holding you as a material witness to a federal crime. I also have reason to believe your life might be in danger."

Both eyebrows went up at that. She blinked through a stream of rising smoke. Bill kept his face frozen in the solid, unmovable mask of federal authority. It was easy for him since he decided that he did not like this woman.

"You can do that? That will hold up with a lawyer and all that?"

"If you'd rather, we can make the case that you were an accomplice in the home invasions. Not hard to convince a judge to let us charge you. Judges don't like coincidences. And you picking a house with a view of a potential murder scene belonging to your ex is a lot to take on faith."

She sat up and smeared the half-smoked cigarette on the table top. The charade was over.

"What do you want?" She sighed.

"You can start by telling us all you know about Tex," Bill said.

5

He left the former Mrs. Blanco for a detailed follow-up with a pair of Boston bureau agents. They assured him they'd have a computer composite drawing in a few hours. It would be based on Kiera Reese's description and checked against what they had from the Xtra Mart video.

The bureau booked him into a Holiday Inn Express. He took a long stinging shower then lay on the bed, willing his mind to rest. He gave up after only a few minutes.

Nancy Valdez answered on the third ring after he got through to her extension past the information tree at Treasury. She didn't recognize his voice at first.

"You sound ragged," she said. It was good to hear her voice again.

"I'm not even sure what day it is," he said.

"Well, it's only two in the afternoon and you don't sound drunk, so I assume this is business," she said.

"I feel hungover and I haven't had a sip." He laughed, punchy, then filled her in on the case so far.

"What is this?" she said.

"I was hoping you'd tell me, Nance." He was punchy. He'd never called her Nance before.

"It sounds like someone interrupted the crew in flagrante. An unexpected party crasher."

"You think someone cowboyed them? Robbed from the thieves?"

"One guy? With a crew this experienced? And with a kid in tow?"

"So, what is it? Karma?" He pressed the bridge of his nose between his thumb and index finger to release the tightening knot there. It didn't work.

"Shit, Bill. I hate to say what it looks like," she said.

"What do you see that I'm not?"

"A vigilante."

"This guy Tex is Batman?" he said, sitting up.

"And Robin. Don't forget the little girl," Nancy said.

***

His phone buzzed, waking him. He could swear he'd only just closed his eyes. The clock on the nightstand read three hours after he'd last looked at it.

"Marquez," he croaked.

"A message from special agent Brompton, sir," a chirpy voice said.

"Go ahead." The sky he could see through the blinds was deep indigo.

"He's sending a car for you. He says it's wheels up in sixty at Minute Man Air Field."

"Okay, okay." He groaned and broke the connection.

The bureau had assigned them a plane. Someone in DC recognized this case was white hot. Recovering a billion or so in funds bilked from private investors would mean headlines. And a few hundred million for the IRS would make whoever recovered it a hero. Bill wondered who'd end up taking the credit once it all cleared.

Bill hobbled to the shower, an old man at thirty-seven.

The young female agent who greeted him in the lobby introduced herself as Mandy. She was fresh out of Quantico and had blood in her eye for promotion. Was he ever that eager? Tired as he was, he admired her calves under the hem of the regulation length skirt as she led him to the car waiting at the turnaround.

She had hot Starbucks and an icy cold orange juice in the cup holders for him. He would have given to her half his kingdom at that point. He sipped the coffee and held the frosty OJ to his forehead. They took off for the airfield.

"We'll need to punch it to make it to Minute Man by the time Agent Brompton's touched down, sir." She expertly shifted lanes to get them onto the right on-ramp for Stow.

Bill balanced the cup to keep the scalding liquid from sloshing from the sip hole onto his pant leg.

"Where's he coming from?" Bill said, eying the inch wide gap between their right fender and the back of a JB Hunt truck they were passing at seventy.

"Bangor. Things have come to a boil. The bureau authorized a Gulfstream. Ever been?" She beamed at the thought, eyes, thank God, locked on the road ahead.

"I haven't."

"Some of them are unbelievable. Seized through

zero tolerance. I was on one last year that belonged to a Sinaloa cartel member. It had a hot tub. A hot tub!"

"There's been a development then?" The coffee was restarting his heart and mind.

"They found the Mercedes. The one taken from the motel in Waltham."

"Where?"

"Maryland," she said and flashed him a wolfish leer.

"Is there more?" He knew there would be.

"You're going to shit." She laughed and quickly added, "Sir."

He believed that he just might as she cut off a Trailways bus to zoom down the exit ramp nearest the airport.

6

"Those fifties were a good catch," Ted Brompton said.

"And a lucky break. Someone said their prayers last night," Bill said.

Bill was settled back in a tufted seat of buttery leather aboard the confiscated luxury jet. The upholstery was so inviting he wanted to sink into it and sleep all week. Starbucks made him jittery but not as awake as he needed to be. He bit the inside of his mouth hard enough to make his eyes water and concentrated on Brompton's words.

"Both bills trace back to an account the SEC was watching when Blanco first came on their radar. They recorded the serial numbers, sprayed them with UV paint and planted them in a stack of bills Blanco's wife withdrew from an account down in Boca."

"The deceased wife?"

"The honey you met up with in Boston. She's a player. Don't you worry; we have plenty to hold her on."

"Surprised the SEC went to all that trouble. Cloak and dagger stuff," Bill said.

Ted snorted. "It was the '90s, bro. Clinton was urging Treasury, IRS and Securities to climb up everyone's asses looking for revenue. He unleashed them."

"The ex-wife give up any more?"

"This invasion crew was after the big enchilada; a key of some kind to all of Blanco's offshore accounts. His rainy day fund. The way the former missus tells it, there was north of a billion five salted away," Ted said with a grin.

"A key?" Bill blinked.

"That's what Blanco told her. But no more than that. It's not an actual key; you can be damned sure of that. He also told her he had numbers for accounts that weren't his own. Other people's money. He could dip into them if he wanted. Whatever this key is, it's a double bonanza and a week in Hawaii for us, Treasury and the tax geeks. Throw in the SEC and FTA too. Careers will be made off of this."

"And she thinks this key was at the lake house?"

"She said he always liked that place best. He built it with the first million he stole. And he was paranoid about keeping too much overseas. Never knew when political winds could change."

"Then maybe our mystery man has this key?"

"That's the smart money."

"She give us a good description of our missing actor?" Bill said.

"Downloaded it on the way from Bangor." Ted handed over a tablet for Bill to look at.

A stern face looked back at Bill from the screen. It was a composite with all the qualities of a high-res photograph. The jawline and mouth matched what he could see under the hoodie in the Xtra Mart video. The eyes, usually lifeless in these recreations, had a predatory look about them. Well-set either side of a nose that had seen a few breaks. It was an intelligent face. Hard but intelligent.

"Facial recognition any help?" Bill said.

"Nada. It's iffy with these visualization programs. The ears and jaw only need to be a little off and we're eye-deeing Liam Neeson. But we may not need it."

"Yeah?"

"Our man got tangled in something in Maryland that the Baltimore PD and VSP are still sorting out."

"VSP?"

"Virginia State Police. We're close behind a possible last known location for this guy. He's ours. He just doesn't know it yet," Ted said with a lupine leer that was a mirror of the grin Agent Mandy had shared with Bill earlier.

Bill wasn't so sure. There was something about that face. Even in the compilation photo he sensed something feral, primal. There was too much about this guy they didn't know.

He kept his thoughts to himself and sank gratefully into the warm depths of the opulent chair and closed his eyes while Ted took a call from DC.

Gunny Leffertz said:
"Luck is no lady. Luck is a bitch. With you one second and gone the next."

7

Merry rested against him as he drove, her breathing soft. He hated to wake her but they were two exits from Roanoke.

Levon Cade drove with eyes shifting to the rear view and to the shoulders of the highway. The wipers slapped at the freezing rain marching in sheets out of the gray dawn light. He watched for the swirling lights of state troopers ahead and behind. By now, someone back in New Market would have found the body of the big man where he'd left it in the entryway of the flower shop. They'd find out who the dead man was. That would lead them to the GMC Sierra that Levon was now piloting south on 81.

He could feel the ring tightening around him. That sense of weight about to fall. He knew to trust that feeling.

The run down from Maine was a long one. It was only a matter of time before the police turned to the feds. And the feds would be putting the pieces together. They'd have an idea of what had happened up at Bellevue. They'd pick up the trail. They'd start stringing together events that would lead them south. He had hours. Maybe less.

Levon weighed speed against caution. He could stay to the highway and build distance between himself and the bodies he'd left behind. Or he could go to ground and wait out the hunt. Going to ground made more sense. If the FBI or multiple agencies were after him it wouldn't be a linear pursuit. They'd get ahead of him.

Simply running was not a solution. That required luck. And he knew he was way past luck. Fresh out of good fortune.

It would be pure D foolishness to underestimate the effort the government would make to find him. Through the fabric of his shirt, Levon's hand touched the lozenge shape that hung around his neck on a silver chain. The flash drive he'd taken from the thieves in Bellevue. It was what they'd gone to Maine to find. They killed for it. And at his hands, they died for it.

Whatever secrets the flash drive held were worth a global hunt by a crew of professionals. And if it was valuable to the thieves then it was valuable to the government. The little drive contained data that might lead to a Solomon's mine of untaxed millions hidden in banks around the world.

Levon had also taken a half million in cash and several millions in cut diamonds from the open vault. The feds wouldn't care about that. They wanted the little plastic stick swinging against his chest. If they got that, and got him, he'd do life on a list of federal charges. A half dozen or more homicides, a kidnapping or two, grand theft, at least three counts of auto theft, assault and whatever else they could tie him to depending on how much of the past two days they figured out. In addition, they could make a case that he was part of the robbery crew and make him an accomplice to all their prior offenses. They were dead. The justice meant for them would fall on him.

He needed to lose the Sierra and find other transport for them. He needed to get off the highway. And there was one more contingency that he didn't want to think about.

Levon's hand dropped to Merry's shoulder to steady her against him on the bench seat as he pulled off the first exit for Roanoke.

***

They left the Sierra on a municipal lot where it wouldn't be noticed. The rain had stopped. The light traffic on the street swished through the slush. Hand in hand, Levon and Merry walked a few blocks to a Hardee's that was open early for breakfast. The place gleamed jewel-like in the muted morning light.

There were kids Merry's age and older in the booths and at the counter. They had book bags and some wore school blazers. Levon took a seat and sent her to the counter to get their order. There would be cameras over the registers. An eleven-year-old girl wouldn't be noticed in the crowd of schoolkids.

Levon rested his boots against the gym bag and overnight bag that contained all he owned. Merry's backpack sat on the bench opposite him. Cartoon characters he didn't recognize capered across the fabric.

Merry came back with a tray loaded with egg and bacon sandwiches, hash brown patties, orange juice and a black coffee. He sipped coffee and watched her eat. There were dark circles under her eyes that he knew weren't from lack of sleep. The sight of her drawn face under strands of rain-drenched hair confirmed the way ahead for both of them.

They hiked down to the main street. No one would take a second look at a girl with a backpack. All the kids on the way to school had book bags. A grown man with a pair of bags would look like he was heading for the bus terminal a few blocks away. Levon found what he was looking for on a strip of stores set back from the street by a small parking lot.

Skyline Cell sold and repaired cell phones and personal devices. They carried satellite phones and prepaid cards for airtime. While Merry played on a display game device, Levon picked out phones and cards. The counter guy woke from a sleepy daze when Levon placed bills on the counter.

"How about a free ball cap?" the counter guy said, pulling down an adjustable cap with the Tracfone logo embroidered in gold against a black panel above the bill.

"No thanks," Levon said.

"It's free. They're gimmes from the company," the guy said and held the cap above the plastic bag he held open on the counter.

Levon shrugged. "Sure. Thanks."

A block away, Levon removed his sodden cap and stuffed it in a trash bin. He fitted the new cap to his head.

***

Merry went into a Rexall with a list from her father. She told the nosy counter woman that her mom and baby brother were homesick and had no one else to pick up the stuff they needed. If the woman wondered why her mother needed bandage strips, packing tape, and three books of postage stamps, she kept it to herself. Merry eyed herself in the HD surveillance image displayed on the monitor above the checkout.

At the post office, Levon filled out a packing label addressed to Gunny Leffertz in Mississippi. He affixed the label to the box containing one of the new satellite phones and then sealed the box all around with the packing tape before placing rows of enough postage stamps to send the package priority. Before all of that he recorded the sat phone's number on the back of a blank customs slip.

Since it was over thirteen ounces Merry took the package into the post office counter. A bored guy with a beard and a mustard stain on his USPS smock postmarked it and plastered Priority Mail stamps on every face of the box before tossing it in a bin with other parcels. If he noted that there was no return address marked on the box he didn't say anything.

"Thank you," Merry said and skipped through the door to the lobby. A buzzer sounded when the door swung open.

"Uh huh," said the bearded guy.

***

Levon and Merry sat on a bench under the shelter of a bus stop. Traffic had picked up as the morning moved on. From their vantage point, Levon could watch the parking lot of a community hospital. Merry dozed, her head down on the backpack in her lap.

A five-year-old Buick Lacrosse pulled onto the lot off the street. It made its way to spaces marked

Emergency Staff only. A slender young woman in royal blue scrubs under a down coat exited the car. She pulled the strap of a gear bag over her shoulder and walked to the entrance under the emergency awning.

Levon touched his daughter's shoulder to wake her. He asked, "What do you do if anything happens?"

"Walk away," she mumbled without raising her head.

"Good girl," he said and lifted the gym bag from the pavement and crossed the street to the hospital lot.

In under sixty seconds he was inside the Lacrosse. Its alarm squawked twice before he cut it off. Car alarms were part of the urban soundtrack. No one paid attention to them. He started the car, which smelled of recent marijuana use, and pulled off the lot. An emergency room nurse would be pulling at least a twelve-hour shift. That was enough lead time to get where he needed to be.

Merry, who had been watching, rose from the bus stop bench to meet him on the lot of a tire store. She carried the overnight in addition to her Adventure Time backpack. They were out of the city and rolling west on a county road.

"Is that mail on the dash?" Levon asked her.

"Yeah. Deborah Ianelli. She lives in Vinton," Merry read from the envelope of a gas company bill.

"We'll send her some cash for the use of the car," he said.

"Okay," she said and reclined her seat until her feet were dangling in the air.

The tires hissed on the wet road as they barreled under the bare limbs of trees arched above. They burst into watery sunlight when the woods gave way to rolling fields dappled with white left from earlier snow.

Merry spoke up when the Lacrosse plunged once more into the shelter of woods. "Daddy?"

"Yes, honey?"

"Why did you buy three of those phones?"

"Well, I was meaning to talk to you about that," he said and swallowed to clear his throat.

8

"I still don't see how this ties in," said Lieutenant Charles Rance of Virginia State Police CID.

Ted Brompton explained, "We're putting the pieces together ourselves." They sat at the counter of the My Way Hi-Way truck stop on 81.

Lieutenant Rance eyed the agent seated by Brompton. The man looked as if he slept in his clothes and was possibly hungover, face gray, hair lank and shoulders bowed where he bent over a plate of scrambled eggs and peppers smothered in hot sauce.

Bill Marquez listened to the exchange. He wolfed his scrambled, washing it down with pulls from a bottomless cup of black coffee. Long stake-outs had taught him something the academy didn't; if you can't get sleep, get calories.

Bill studied Rance once the big statie turned away. Guy was ex-military for sure. Skin dark as the coffee Bill was slamming down. Gray creeping in on the short-back-and-sides-cut hair, otherwise it was impossible to nail down the guy's age. Desert Storm vet maybe. The statie wore his tailored blue suit like a uniform; knife-edge creases, dazzling white shirt and conservative pale blue tie with a little pair of gold handcuffs pinning it in place. Bill felt like an unmade bed around a guy like this.

"So, a home invasion homicide in Maine two days ago ties into a homicide here in New Market last night?" Rance said, trying to keep up with Agent Brompton's timeline.

"That's the working theory. Can you share what you have?" Brompton smiled professionally.

Rance flipped open a notepad and read:

"Calvin Thomas Shepherd is the deceased. Multiple gunshots. Time of death sometime after midnight last night. He has a record but no convictions in Maryland and New Jersey. Assault mostly. Whoever shot him either used a revolver or picked up their brass. They worked close, too. CSI said there were powder burns on Shepherd's clothes."

Ted said, "He's tied in with a crew in Baltimore. We found three of them dead in a bar in Towson. Killed sometime yesterday afternoon."

"Dawson," Bill said around a mouthful of eggs and peppers.

"Right. How did Shepherd get here? You find a car?" Ted said.

"He had no keys on him. Maybe someone drove him here and killed him," the lieutenant said, flipping his pad closed.

"Or killed him and took his ride." Bill pushed the empty plate from him and jabbed a finger down at his empty mug for a wandering waitress to see.

"Did Baltimore give us a list of cars in Shepherd's name?" Ted said, turning his stool to Bill.

Bill touched his smartphone, scrolling until he found what he wanted. He picked the phone up and squinted, eyelids still gritty.

"A GMC Sierra. Forest Green. This year's model. Maryland plate. GXR-977."

"Then that's what he's driving," Ted said to the statie.

"That's what who is driving?" Rance said.

"That's what we'd like to know," Bill watched with greedy eyes as the waitress loaded up his mug.

The lieutenant called his superiors who put a BOLO out for the Sierra. As they walked out to their cars, he promised the two FBI agents to send along all the initial reports on Shepherd. He didn't expect any revelations.

Ted shrugged. "Rained like hell last night."

The agents thanked him and picked their way between puddles to the bureau car they'd gotten from the Baltimore office.

Gunny Leffertz said:
"Move away from your attacker. Distance is your friend. Only break up your unit when pursuit is close."

9

Merry slept most of the drive and when awake spoke only when spoken to. She was angry and hurt over what he had to tell her, the hard decision he was forced to make.

"You wanted to visit Gunny and Joyce."

She turned to the window, voice breaking. "With you. But you won't be there."

"I don't want it to be this way, honey."

"Then keep driving. Just drive till we both get there."

"I can't. I explained why I can't."

"I don't want to go alone."

"And I don't like the idea either. This is the best way. The only way. I'm all out of options. You have to be brave."

She wouldn't answer him. They rode in silence.

It was after midnight when Levon pulled into the lot of the America's Best Value Inn in Murphysboro, Illinois. The drive from Virginia had taken fourteen hours. Two hours added to the straight through drive because he stuck to county roads until they were well into Tennessee. He got them on Route 40 at Knoxville around three in the afternoon.

Levon checked himself into a single room using the story that his wife kicked him out of the house. His father-in-law, a mean son of a bitch, was over to the house. He didn't have time to get his wallet, he just got his ass the hell out of there. A buddy lent him a couple hundred.

"Whydn't you stay with your buddy?" the guy at the desk asked more out of idle curiosity and desire for conversation on a slow night.

"He's married to my wife's sister," Levon said, shit-eating grin in place.

The guy barked at that and slid the room card to him.

After checking for cameras Levon met Merry at a back exit. There were none and he let her in. They used the stairs to reach the room. Without a word she locked herself in the bathroom. He lay back on the bedcovers to close his eyes for a second. He could hear the shower running.

That was the last thing he heard before he awakened to the drag and boom of truck traffic out on the highway. Sunlight was streaming in through a gap in the drapes. Merry was asleep in an armchair pulled up close in front of the TV, curled in a ball under a quilt. A smiling man and woman on the TV were making something in a dream kitchen, clean white aprons worn over immaculate clothes. The volume was reduced to a sibilant mutter.

He took a long shower, thought about shaving and decided that it should wait.

When he came out of the bathroom, Merry had moved to the bed. She lay under the covers, facing the window, her back to him.

Levon dressed and went to see about getting them breakfast.

***

He walked to an IHOP down the road from the hotel. The Lacrosse was backed into a space at the rear of the lot behind the America's Best. It wouldn't draw attention to itself. Cheaters parked that way to hide their plates.

Merry was as he left her when he got back with two plastic bags of take-out waffles in clamshell containers. The smell was enough to lure her out from under the covers. She ate in silence, digging into a stack of strawberry shortcake waffles. She nodded when he held up maple syrup packets.

She wasn't angry, wasn't sullen. When she did look at him it was with an expression of heartbreaking sadness. He knew she was hurting at the idea of them separating. He couldn't help but read into it a resentment about all that he'd put her through since they left Huntsville almost a year ago.

Levon knew his little girl would never hold that against him. Since her mother died, Merry accepted that life was capable of cruel surprise. A hard thing for an eleven-year-old to deal with, even harder for Levon to take on. A father was supposed to shield his child from trouble, not bring more on. And she had no idea of half of the trouble he invited into their lives when he'd agreed to go hunting for Jim Wiley's daughter. He was a wanted man. The only grandparents Merry knew were dead. They lived on the road, changing names and homes.

His decision was a hard one to make. But it was

best for her and that's all that mattered.

Even though these next few days would not be the happiest between them, they were still precious to him. Waiting in this hotel room, eating take-out and watching TV wasn't anyone's idea of quality time. But they were together and that would have to be enough for him and, hopefully, enough for Merry when she looked back on it.

For now, they were waiting out the days until Gunny got the package he'd mailed the day before.

10

After seventy-two near-straight hours of wakeful-
ness, Bill felt like he was watching the landscape go
by through the wrong end of a telescope. He wished
he could be the next FBI agent shot in the line of duty
just so he'd have permission to lie down.

"You look like shit," Ted said, eying him from
behind wheel.

"I feel like shit," he replied, drooping against his
shoulder strap.

"Lexington is coming up. I'm dropping you off
for some rack time. There's nothing going on right
now anyway."

Bill could only nod. Even that motion was a supreme effort.

Ted dumped him off at a Day's Inn close to the
highway.

Ted called from the car, "Take a shower. Get your
clothes pressed. And get some sleep. I can give you
six hours max."

Bill waved. He slumped toward the entrance,
bag slung over his shoulder. The automatic doors

hissed open and warm, welcoming canned air swept over him from within. He thought he heard angels singing but it was only Abba on the lobby PA system.

***

Showered and wrapped in a towel, Bill lay back atop the covers on his economy double bed and punched in the numbers to reach Nancy Valdez at Treasury. He wasn't sure why he was calling her. All he knew was that, beat as he was, he wouldn't be able to sleep without talking to her. She was his confessor and sleep was his communion. The nuns would approve of that analogy, he thought as he listened to the Brahms piano concerto that served as hold music for the T-men.

"They've brought me in on this Maine thing," Nancy told him once he reached her.

"Yeah?"

"Same as the bureau brought you in. My background on this. They're putting together a cross-agency task force. A hump from DHS is taking lead."

"What's Homeland's interest here?" Bill said.

"They found a pickup truck up at the Maine site registered to the Mitchell Roeder alias. An automatic rifle and lots of ammo were found concealed in it. That's all they need to claim domestic terrorism."

"Brompton's not going to be happy about that."

"Who's that?"

"Agent I'm working under. He thinks he's lead on this."

She said, "He's not lead as of an hour ago. The Blanco ex is talking a blue streak to save her ass. I don't have details but she swears that whatever the guys in this crew were looking for was in the Maine house. I have to bite my tongue to keep from saying 'told you so.'"

"What about Tex? Roeder? The guy on the run?" he said with a yawn.

"She says he wasn't with the crew. Just the right guy showing up at the wrong time. She followed him to Waltham and braced him. She thought, as Blanco's only surviving ex, she was entitled to a piece of whatever he got away with."

"She know his real name? Where he's heading?"

"She knew him as Mitch Roeder from Arkansas. That matches a—" He heard her tapping keys. "—a Mitchell Jennings Roeder, born in Jonesboro. Born in '85. Died in a car accident aged four. It's a professional identity appropriation. This guy either paid a lot or had help."

"But he is a southern boy."

"Well, according to the ex he is. Of course, she's Boston born. Anyone south of Philadelphia sounds like Reba McEntire to her. Guy could be from anywhere from Indiana to the Florida Keys. And the composite isn't much good."

"A bulletproof false ID," Bill said, "and he knows how to defeat facial recognition and elude a combined state, local and federal dragnet. And he brought down a crew of badasses all by himself. Think he's one of us? Or was one of us?"

"Does sound like he has skills, doesn't it?" Nancy said.

"Or former military."

"You sound tired." The cynical cool had melted from her voice.

"You have no idea," he said and watched the ceiling swimming in and out of focus.

"The world will still be here when you wake up."

"That's what I'm afraid of, Nancy."

"Good night, Bill."

He was already gone, the cell phone tumbling from his hand to the carpet.

11

It was flurrying snow when the taxi pulled up under the apron at the entrance of the America's Best. A big guy in work boots squeezed his way into the cramped confines of the minivan's rear seat. The driver eyeballed the guy in the rearview. He looked like he was dressed to go deer hunting. Or, with a heavy growth of beard on his jaw, maybe fresh back from a deer camp.

"Where to?" the driver said.

"You tell me . . . Phil," the big man said, leaning forward to read the driver's name off the ID plate on dash.

"What's the supposed to mean?" said the driver whose name was not Phil. That was his cousin who owned the hack and allowed a couple of family members to rack up hours behind the wheel, though that was not strictly legal. In truth, it was entirely illegal.

"I'm new in town. I don't know where to go." With an easy smile, the big man rested back on the seat.

"And I'm supposed to tell you?" not-Phil said,

studying his passenger in the reflection.

The big guy leaned forward, a fifty folded between his fingers. "Just a few helpful suggestions, you being a local."

"Help me out, son. Are you thirsty or are you lonely?" Not-Phil took the fifty and slipped it into the breast pocket of his shirt.

"Lonely."

"I know just the place," not-Phil, said and put the mini in gear to roll out toward the highway to enter the stream of golden lights flowing past in the winter gloom.

***

The place was a single home in what was once a blue-collar neighborhood in nearby Carbondale. The house glowed amber under twinkle lights left up long after Christmas. They gave off a dismal rather than festive effect. A four bedroom with a three-car carport on a half-acre lot enclosed by cyclone fencing. Two Dobermans trotted around the yard. The snow was mottled with their feces.

A train passed by in the dark close enough that Levon could hear the clank of the coupler heads as it slowed into a yard.

The driver handed over his business card.

"For the drive back," not-Phil said.

"Thanks." Levon let him keep the fifty for a twenty dollar fare.

A waist-high gate opened from the sidewalk onto a paved walkway lined either side with cyclone fencing creating a lane all the way to the front door. The two dogs loped beside him, heads held low, sniffing through the links. Not a sound out of either of them.

They were biters.

At the barred front door he pressed a doorbell. A voice spoke from an intercom. A man's voice. Gruff.

"What house are you looking for?"

"This one," Levon said and held up the cab driver's business card to the lens of the camera mounted above the door inside a mirrored plastic dome.

There was a buzz and a click and Levon turned the knob and entered.

The impression of a typical suburban home ended once he was inside. A cramped foyer with paneled walls and a single steel door mounted to the left. To his right was an opening that resembled a teller's booth in a bank. It was fronted by a pane of Lexan with a pay slot built in at the bottom. The once-clear plastic was yellowed by years of nicotine. An immensely fat man sat behind the pane in a brightly lit room no bigger than a closet. He wore suspenders over a shirt decorated with red roses. A half-eaten apple pie sat by him on a narrow counter. He stuck a fork in the crust. He inclined his head to look at Levon through glasses perched on the end of his nose.

"I don't know you."

The same razor-gargling voice Levon had heard over the intercom.

"I've never been here before," Levon said.

"Andy sent you?" That must have been not-Phil's real name.

"He drove me here. Just dropped me off."

"You're not a cop. I know all the cops," the fat man said without a trace of accusation in his tone.

"Me? A cop?" Levon acted as if the suggestion was both amusing and ludicrous.

"There's a menu on the wall. Prices are not negotiable." The fat man poked a sausage finger to his right.

Levon stepped closer to read a printed page enclosed in a plastic sheet that was tacked to the paneling. It listed, in graphic and unmistakable terms, the services offered and the prices demanded. Costs went all the way to five hundred dollars. A notice in the bottom in yellow highlight stated that "each additional party to any of the above services requires an additional charge equal to the price of the selected service."

"You want a white girl? A black one? We have an Asian girl but you'll have to wait for her," the fat man announced through the slot.

Levon stepped back to the Lexan and stood to one side of the waist-high cash slot.

"I was looking for something not on the menu," Levon said.

The fat man glanced away from his pie, his eyes narrowed. His mouth turned down in a wet frown.

"I don't want any trouble and I'm not going to have any."

"Slow down. It's not like whatever you're thinking it is," Levon said, smiling easy, hands held up before him.

"Then what is it?"

"I need papers. Eye-dee. They don't have to be the best. Just enough to get me where I'm going," Levon said.

"Now's when I ask you if you're cop. Are you a cop?"

"Thought you knew all the cops."

"All the cops in the county. Not all the cops in

the state."

"I'm not a cop. State, federal or otherwise. I'm just a guy who needs to be someone else for a while. And I need it quick."

"Quick is expensive," the fat man said, eyeing Levon's workman clothes.

Levon counted out five hundred in fifties and twenties and placed them on the smooth sill of the cash slot. The fat man grasped them, all interest in the pie forgotten. He tugged on the bills but Levon maintained his grip.

"Driver's license, any state. And something with a matching address. Utility bill or like that. And an insurance company card," Levon said, meeting the other man's piggy eyes through the hazed pane.

"Bring twice this much back tomorrow."

Levon released his grip. The fat man plucked the bills away.

"What time?"

"We open at one in the afternoon. I should have what you need by then."

Levon nodded.

"What about a picture?" the fat man said.

Levon placed a flat square of plastic the size of a postage stamp on the counter and slid it through the slot. It was the photo cut from his Mitch Roeder driver's license.

"This do?"

"Sure. You staying awhile? Your money's good here," the fat man said, nodded toward the menu.

"Maybe another time. Buzz me out," Levon said and stepped out into the cold.

12

Bill Marquez was rested and restless. Two days of doubling back, re-reading notes, re-questioning sources, left him sour. He was ready to punch a hole in a wall.

Mitch Roeder's, AKA Tex, trail died in Roanoke.

They found the GMC truck that belonged to Calvin Shepherd on a city lot. There was a report from Roanoke PD of a stolen Buick taken off a hospital lot. Could be their man. If it was he had a twelve-hour head start and could be in any one of seven states by now.

Ted Brompton got Bill his own car and sent him back upstream to talk to witnesses. The night counter guy at the Dogwood in New Market critiqued the composite image. He'd gotten a good look at the guy. Described, as best he could, the little girl, too. Witness descriptions of kids weren't worth shit generally. Men really never looked at kids unless they were pervs. Women were better at descriptions of children; they noticed things like eye color and clothing.

The counter guy remembered that Roeder went outside. Pointed to the front door of the Dogwood, the street sunny now with afternoon light.

"But it was pissing rain that night. Said he wanted a smoke. He came back inside after a little bit, paid for the check with a twenty and took the little girl out with him."

That would have been when Shepherd was killed only a few doors away.

"Anyone else here that night?" Bill asked.

"Someone was in one of the other booths. A local, I think. A regular. Give me a second and I'll remember," the counter guy said, nodding to an empty booth behind Bill.

"Anyone else you do remember?"

"Two deputies. Howard Chase and Barry Tillotson. But they had their backs to the guy the whole time. We were talking basketball," the counter guy said.

"I'll talk to them anyway. You never know." Bill went for his wallet to pay for the tuna sandwich and Coke he ordered. The counter guy waved him off.

"Take it off my taxes," he joked.

Bill faked a chuckle and turned to leave.

"Hey, can we start using the ladies room again?" the guy said, gesturing to the door at the back of the place. There was yellow crime scene tape across the opening of a room marked GALS.

Bill shrugged. "Sure. We got all we can out of there."

Bill drove over to the sheriff's annex and caught the two deputies clocking in for the four to midnight. Neither of them had seen a damned thing. Had their backs to the perp the whole time. One of them actually used the word "perp."

Everyone watches too goddamn much television, Bill thought as he backed the bureau Chevy out from the row of black and tan county cars.

He pulled onto 81 and drove north toward DC. Tex's possible route down from New Haven was starting to come together and they had gathered footage from bridges, toll booths and red light cameras. More videos were trickling in from gas stations, discount stores and fast food drive-thrus. There was a team reviewing video. A model was being built backtracking Tex and his daughter all the way back to Lake Whatsis in Maine.

Ted wanted him to wrangle the team and apply pressure for results. It was bureaucratic gravity in effect. DHS was applying pressure to Ted to bring them some good news. Ted was raining shit down on every agent below him.

The current administration was positively sex-mad for homegrown terrorists of the non-Islamic variety. They were always making a case for the danger of militias and white supremacy groups. Anyone in fed law enforcement knew this was boogeyman stuff. The only militias Bill had ever seen were weekend warriors out playing Rambo in the woods. Tubby guys who got bored reenacting Civil War battles and wanted to play with semi-automatic rifles instead of muskets.

And the racist groups were even sadder. They mostly spent their time in court fighting for permits to join parades or set up booths at state fairs. When they weren't doing that they were making videos for their web sites. It was Bill's opinion that they should run those videos during the Super Bowl and let the whole country see what a bunch of pathetic assholes these master race dickheads were.

To get the task force that the bureau and Treasury wanted, Ted let the political animals at Homeland think the guy they were chasing was the next Timothy McVeigh. That allowed them to tap the IRS and the NSA for Intel. Hell, the IRS had four times the agents that the G-men and T-men had.

It was all bullshit anyway. Whoever Tex was, he was a loner. Except for the little girl, of course. But Bill had a gut feeling this guy was more dangerous than a whole compound of survivalist crazies.

When Nancy Valdez called, he shared this with her over the car phone.

"Look at the way he's played us. Slipped the knot like a pro. Add that to the shit pile of corpses he left in Maine and whatever he got himself into with that Baltimore crew," Bill told her as he drove north toward the beltway.

"He's trained and he's smart. And if the former Mrs. Blanco is right he has the keys to the national debt of Bolivia," Nancy said from the speaker on the dash.

"I don't hear office noise."

"I'm not in the office."

"Are you home?" he asked.

"Next you're going to ask me what I'm wearing." He could hear her smile when she said it.

"I'm guessing a Glock."

"Fuck you. It's a Sig. I wouldn't touch a Glock with your dick."

"Whoa, lady! This is a government line you're on."

"So, where you heading next?"

"Just did my last interview. They called me back

to Quantico. Due diligence and background with the task force," Bill said.

"That's where they have me. I'm heading out the door right now," she said, her voice bright.

"I'll see you there then."

"See you."

Bill tabbed END CALL on the dash monitor. A car honked its horn and flashed high beams as he passed it on the right. He looked at the display. He was doing ninety-two in a sixty zone.

ABOUT THE AUTHOR

Born and raised in Philadelphia, Chuck Dixon worked a variety of jobs from driving an ice cream truck to working graveyard at a 7-11 before trying his hand as a writer. After a brief sojourn in children's books he turned to his childhood love of comic books. In his thirty years as a writer for Marvel, DC Comics and other publishers, Chuck built a reputation as a prolific and versatile freelancer working on a wide variety titles and genres from Conan the Barbarian to SpongeBob SquarePants. His graphic novel adaptation of J.R.R. Tolkien's The Hobbit continues to be an international bestseller translated into fifty languages. He is the co-creator (with Graham Nolan) of the Batman villain Bane, the first enduring member added to the Dark Knight's rogue's gallery in forty years. He was also one of the seminal writers responsible for the continuing popularity of Marvel Comics' The Punisher.

After making his name in comics, Chuck moved to prose in 2011 and has since written over twenty novels, mostly in the action-thriller genre with a few side-trips to horror, hardboiled noir and western. The transition from the comics form to prose has been a life-altering event for him. As Chuck says, "writing a comic is like getting on a roller coaster while writing a novel is more like a long car trip with a bunch of people you'll learn to hate." His Levon Cade novels are currently in production as a television series from Sylvester Stallone's Balboa Productions. He currently lives in central Florida and, no, he does not miss the snow.

Made in United States
Troutdale, OR
11/04/2023

14293662R00094